GRIMMS' FAIRY TALES

GRIMM'S FAIRY TALES

VOLUME ONE

Translated by Edgar Taylor
Illustrated by George Cruikshank

Reproduced in facsimile from the
first English edition

LONDON
THE SCOLAR PRESS
1977

Printed and published in Great Britain by
The Scolar Press Ltd, Ilkley, Yorkshire
and 39 Great Russell Street, London WC1

ISBN 0 85967 421 5

The first volume of fairy tales collected by the philologists Jacob and Wilhelm Grimm appeared in Germany in 1812 as *Kinder-und Hausmärchen*, and the second was published posthumously in 1815. Edgar Taylor, with the support of Sir Walter Scott, prepared a translation of the first volume, which was issued with enchanting illustrations by George Cruikshank in 1823 under the title *German Popular Stories*. Such was its success that a second volume, also illustrated by Cruikshank, followed in 1826.

Taylor's edition, with its clear and simple rendering of the orally collected originals, remains the most authentic and satisfying. For students of folklore, parents and children, this facsimile provides an opportunity to read the *Fairy Tales* as the Brothers Grimm intended them to be read.

GERMAN POPULAR STORIES,

&c.

"Now you must imagine me to sit by a good fire, amongst a companye of good fellowes, over a well spiced wassel bowle of Christmas ale, telling of these merrie tales which hereafter followe."—*Pref. to Hist. of " Tom Thumbe the Little."*—1621.

GERMAN POPULAR STORIES,

Translated from the

Kinder und Haus-Märchen,

COLLECTED BY

M. M. GRIMM,

From Oral Tradition.

G. Cruikshank fec.t

Published by C. Baldwyn, Newgate Street.

LONDON,

1823.

PREFACE.

———◆———

THE Translators were first induced to compile this little work by the eager relish with which a few of the tales were received by the young friends to whom they were narrated. In this feeling the Translators, however, do not hesitate to avow their own participation. Popular fictions and traditions are somewhat gone out of fashion ; yet most will own them to be associated with the brightest recollections of their youth. They are, like the Christmas Pantomimes, ostensibly brought forth to tickle the palate of the young, but often received with as keen an appetite by those of graver years.

There is, at least, a debt of gratitude due to these ancient friends and comforters. To follow the words of the author from whom the motto in the title-page is selected, " They have been the revivers of drowzy age at midnight ; old and young have with such tales chimed mattins till the cock

a 2

crew in the morning; batchelors and maides have compassed the Christmas fire-block till the curfew bell rang candle out; the old shepheard and the young plow-boy after their daye's labor, have carold out the same to make them merrye with; and who but they have made long nightes seem short, and heavy toyles easie ?"

But the amusement of the hour was not the translators' only object. The rich collection from which the following tales are selected, is very interesting in a literary point of view, as affording a new proof of the wide and early diffusion of these gay creations of the imagination, apparently flowing from some great and mysterious fountain head, whence Calmuck, Russian, Celt, Scandinavian, and German, in their various ramifications, have imbibed their earliest lessons of moral instruction.

The popular tales of England have been too much neglected. They are nearly discarded from the libraries of childhood. Philosophy is made the companion of the nursery : we have lisping chemists and leading-string mathematicians : this is the age of reason, not of imagination; and the loveliest dreams of fairy innocence are considered as vain and frivolous. Much might be urged against this rigid and philosophic (or rather unphilosophic) exclusion of works of fancy and fiction.

Our imagination is surely as susceptible of improvement by eoercise, as our judgement or our memory; and so long as such fictions only are presented to the young mind as do not interfere with the important department of moral education, a beneficial effect must be produced by the pleasurable employment of a faculty in which so much of our happiness in every period of life consists.

It is, however, probably owing merely to accidental causes that some countries have carefully preserved their ancient stores of fiction, while here they have been suffered to pass to oblivion or corruption, notwithstanding the patriotic example of a few such names as Hearne, Spelman, and Le Neve, who did not disdain to turn towards them the light of their carefully trimmed lamp, scanty and ill-furnished as it often was. A very interesting and ingenious article in the *Quarterly Review*, (No. xli.) to which the Translators readily acknowledge their particular obligations, recently attracted attention to the subject, and has shown how wide a field is open, interesting to the antiquarian as well as to the reader who only seeks amusement.

The collection from which the following Tales are taken is one of great extent, obtained for the

a 3

most part from the mouths of German peasants by the indefatigable exertions of John and William Grimm, brothers in kindred and taste.—The result of their labours ought to be peculiarly interesting to English readers, inasmuch as many of their national tales are proved to be of the highest Northern antiquity, and common to the parallel classes of society in countries whose populations have been long and widely disjoined. Strange to say, " Jack, commonly called the Giant-killer, and Thomas Thumb," as the reviewer observes, " landed in England from the very same hulls and war ships which conveyed Hengist and Horsa, and Ebba the Saxon." Who would have expected that Whittington and his Cat, whose identity and London citizenship appeared so certain ;—Tom Thumb, whose parentage Hearne had traced, and whose monumental honours were the boast of Lincoln ; — or the Giant-destroyer of Tylney, whose bones were supposed to moulder in his native village in Norfolk, should be equally renowned among the humblest inhabitants of Munster and Paderborn ?

A careful comparison would probably establish many other coincidences. The sports and songs of children, to which MM. Grimm have directed considerable attention, often excite surprise at their striking resemblance to the usages of our own country. We wish, with Leucadio Doblado, speaking of Spanish popular sports, " that anti- quarians were a more jovial and volatile race, and that some one would trace up these amusements to their common source," if such a thing were possible, or at any rate would point out their af- finities. A remarkable coincidence occurs in the German song to the Lady-bird or " Marien-würm- chen." The second verse alone has been preserved in England ; but it is singular that the burthen of the song should have been so long preserved in countries whose inhabitants have been so com- pletely separated. The whole song, which is to be found in *Wunderhorn*, i. 235, may be thus trans- lated :

> Lady-bird ! Lady-bird ! pretty one ! stay !
> Come sit on my finger, so happy and gay ;
>   With me shall no mischief betide thee ;
> No harm would I do thee, no foeman is near,
> I only would gaze on thy beauties so dear,
>   Those beautiful winglets beside thee.

> Lady-bird ! Lady-bird ! fly away home !
> Thy house is a-fire, thy children will roam ;
>   List ! list ! to their cry and bewailing :
> The pitiless spider is weaving their doom,
> Then, Lady-bird ! Lady-bird ! fly away home !
>   Hark ! hark ! to thy children's bewailing.

Fly back again, back again, Lady-bird dear !
Thy neighbours will merrily welcome thee here ;
    With them shall no perils attend thee :
They'll guard thee so safely from danger or care,
They'll gaze on thy beautiful winglets so fair,
    And comfort, and love, and befriend thee.

The valuable notes and dissertations added by
MM. Grimm to their work, have principally for
their object to establish the connexion between
many of these traditions and the ancient mytho-
logical fables of the Scandinavian and Teutonic
nations. " In these popular stories," they are
sanguine enough to believe, "is concealed the
pure and primitive mythology of the Teutons,
which has been considered as lost for ever ; and
they are convinced, that if such researches are continued in the different districts of Germany, the
traditions of this nature which are now neglected,
will change into treasures of incredible worth, and
assist in affording a new basis for the study of the
origin of their ancient poetical fictions." On these
points their illustrations, though sometimes over-
strained, are often highly interesting and satisfac-
tory. Perhaps more attention might have been
directed to illustrate the singular admixture of
Oriental incidents of fairy and romance, with the
ruder features of Northern fable ; and particularly

to inform us how far the well-known vehicles of the lighter Southern fictions were current at an early period in Germany. It often seems difficult to account for the currency, among the peasantry on the shores of the Baltic and the forests of the Hartz, of fictions which would seem to belong to the Entertainments of the Arabians, yet involved in legends referable to the highest Teutonic origin.

But it is curious to observe that this connexion between the popular tales of remote and uncon-nected regions, is equally remarkable in the rich-est collection of traditionary narrative which any country can boast; we mean the " *Pentamerone, overo Trattenemiento de li Piccerille,*" ('Fun for the Little Ones,') published by Giov. Battista Ba-sile, very early in the 17th century, from the old stories current among the Neapolitans. It is sin-gular that the German and the Neapolitan tales (though the latter were till lately quite unknown to foreigners, and never translated out of the Italian tongues,) bear the strongest and most minute resemblances. The French fairy tales, that have become so popular, were chiefly taken from " *The Nights (Notti piacevoli) of Strapparola,*" published first in 1550 ; but in his collection such fictions occupy no prominent and apparently only an accidental station, the bulk of the tales being of what may be called the Classical Italian School. The *Pentamerone* was drawn from original sources, and probably compiled without any knowledge of Strapparola, although the latter is precedent in date. The two works have only four pieces in common. Mr. Dunlop would add greatly to the value of his excellent work on Fiction, if he would include in his inquiries this most interesting branch of popular entertainment, to which Sir Walter Scott has already pointed in his notes to " *The Lady of the Lake.*"

Among the most pleasing of the German tales are those in which animals support the lead- ing characters. They are perhaps more vene- rable in their origin than the heroic and fairy tales. They are not only amusing by their playful and dramatic character, but instructive by the pu- rity of their morality. None bear more strongly the impress of a remote Eastern original, both in their principles and their form of conveying in- struction. Justice always prevails, active talent is every where successful, the amiable and gene- rous qualities are brought forward to excite the sympathies of the reader, and in the end are con- stantly rewarded by triumph over lawless power. It will be observed as a peculiarity of the Ger- man fables, that they introduce even inanimate

objects among their actors, a circumstance sometimes attended with considerable effect. Even
the sun, the moon, and the winds, form part of
the *dramatis personæ*.

The Translators can do little more than direct the attention of the curious reader to the
source whence they have selected their mate-
rials. The nature and immediate design of the
present publication exclude the introduction of
some of those stories which would, in a literary
point of view, be most curious. With a view to
variety, they have wished rather to avoid than
to select those, the leading incidents of which are
already familiar to the English reader, and have
therefore often deprived themselves of the interest
which comparison would afford. There were also
many stories of great merit, and tending highly to
the elucidation of ancient mythology, customs, and
opinions, which the scrupulous fastidiousness of
modern taste, especially in works likely to attract
the attention of youth, warned them to pass by.
If they should ever be encouraged to resume their
task, they might undertake it with different and
more serious objects. In those tales which they
have selected they had proposed to make no alteration whatever ; but in a few instances they
have been compelled to depart in some degree

from their purpose. They have, however, endeavoured to notice these variations in the notes, and in most cases the alteration consists merely in the curtailment of adventures or circumstances not affecting the main plot or character of the story.

A few brief notes are added ; but the Translators trust it will always be borne in mind, that their little work makes no literary pretensions ; that its immediate design precludes the subjects most attractive as matters of research ; and that professedly critical dissertations would therefore be out of place. Their object in what they have done in this department, has been merely to direct attention to a subject little noticed, and to point, however imperfectly, at a source of interesting and amusing inquiry.

G. Cruikshank fect.

POPULAR STORIES.

HANS IN LUCK.

HANS had served his master seven years, and at last said to him, " Master, my time is up, I should like to go home and see my mother; so give me my wages." And the master said, " You have been a faithful and good servant, so your pay shall be handsome." Then he gave him a piece of silver that was as big as his head.

Hans took out his pocket-handkerchief, put the piece of silver into it, threw it over his shoulder, and jogged off homewards. As he went lazily on, dragging one foot after another, a man came in sight, trotting along gaily on a capital horse. " Ah!" said Hans aloud, " what a fine thing it is to ride on horseback!

there he sits as if he was at home in his chair; he trips against no stones, spares his shoes, and yet gets on he hardly knows how." The horseman heard this, and said, "Well, Hans, why do you go on foot then?" "Ah!" said he, " I have this load to carry; to be sure it is silver, but it is so heavy that I can't hold up my head, and it hurts my shoulder sadly." " What do you say to changing?" said the horseman; " I will give you my horse, and you shall give me the silver." " With all my heart," said Hans: " but I tell you one thing,—you'll have a weary task to drag it along." The horseman got off, took the silver, helped Hans up, gave him the bridle into his hand, and said, " When you want to go very fast, you must smack your lips loud, and cry ' Jip.' "

Hans was delighted as he sat on the horse, and rode merrily on. After a time he thought he should like to go a little faster, so he smacked his lips, and cried " Jip." Away went the horse full gallop; and before Hans knew what he was about, he was thrown off, and lay in a ditch by the road side; and his horse would have run off, if a shepherd who was coming by, driving a cow, had not stopt it. Hans soon came to himself, and got upon his legs again. He was sadly vexed, and said to the shepherd, " This riding is no joke when a man gets on a beast like this, that stumbles and flings him off as if he would break his neck. However, I'm off now once for all: I like your cow a great deal better; one can walk along at one's leisure behind her, and have milk, butter, and cheese, every day into the bargain. What would I give to have such a cow !" " Well," said the shepherd, " if you are so fond of her, I will change my cow for your horse." " Done !" said Hans merrily. The shepherd jumped upon the horse, and away he rode.

Hans drove off his cow quietly, and thought his bargain a very lucky one. " If I have only a piece of bread (and I certainly shall be able to get that), I can, whenever I like, eat my butter and cheese with it; and when I am thirsty I can milk my cow and drink the milk: what can I wish for more ?" When he came to an inn, he halted, ate up all his bread, and gave away his last penny for a glass of beer: then he drove his cow towards his mother's village; and the heat grew greater as noon came on, till at last he found himself on a wide heath that would take him more than an hour to cross, and he began to be so hot and parched that his tongue clave to the roof of his mouth. "I can find a cure for this," thought he; "now will I milk my cow and quench my thirst;" so he tied her to the stump of a tree, and held his leathern cap to milk into; but not a drop was to be had.

While he was trying his luck and managing the matter very clumsily, the uneasy beast gave him a kick on the head that knocked him down, and there he lay a long while senseless. Luckily a butcher soon came by driving a pig in a wheel-barrow. "What is the matter with you?" said the butcher as he helped him up. Hans told him what had happened, and the butcher gave him a flask, saying, "There, drink and refresh yourself; your cow will give you no milk, she is an old beast good for nothing but the slaughter-house." "Alas, alas!" said Hans, "who would have thought it? If I kill her, what will she be good for? I hate cow-beef, it is not tender enough for me. If it were a pig now, one could do something with it, it would at any rate make some sausages." " Well," said the butcher, " to please you, I'll change, and give you the pig for the cow." " Heaven reward you for your kindness!" said Hans as he gave the butcher the cow, and took the pig off the wheel-barrow, and drove it off, holding it by the string that was tied to its leg.

So on he jogged, and all seemed now to go right with him; he had met with some misfortunes, to be sure; but he was now well re-paid for all. The next person he met was a countryman carrying a fine white goose under his arm. The countryman stopped to ask what was o'clock; and Hans told him all his luck, and how he had made so many good bargains. The countryman said he was going to take the goose to a christening; " Feel," said he, " how heavy it is, and yet it is only eight weeks old. Whoever roasts and eats it may cut plenty of fat off it, it has lived so well!" " You're right," said Hans as he weighed it in his hand; " but my pig is no trifle." Meantime the country-man began to look grave, and shook his head.

" Hark ye," said he, "my good friend; your pig may get you into a scrape; in the village I just come from, the squire has had a pig stolen out of his stye. I was dreadfully afraid, when I saw you, that you had got the squire's pig; it will be a bad job if they catch you; the least they'll do, will be to throw you into the horse-pond."

Poor Hans was sadly frightened. " Good man," cried he, "pray get me out of this scrape; you know this country better than I, take my pig and give me the goose." " I ought to have something into the bargain," said the country-man; " however, I will not bear hard upon you, as you are in trouble." Then he took the string in his hand, and drove off the pig by a side path; while Hans went on the way home-wards free from care. "After all," thought he, " I have the best of the bargain: first there will be a capital roast; then the fat will find me in goose grease for six months; and then there are all the beautiful white feathers; I will put them into my pillow, and then I am sure I shall sleep soundly without rocking. How happy my mother will be!"

As he came to the last village, he saw a scissar-grinder, with his wheel, working away, and singing

O'er hill and o'er dale so happy I roam,
Work light and live well, all the world is my home;
Who so blythe, so merry as I?

Hans stood looking for a while, and at last said, " You must be well off, master grinder, you seem so happy at your work." " Yes," said the other, " mine is a golden trade; a good grinder never puts his hand in his pocket with-out finding money in it:—but where did you get that beautiful goose?" " I did not buy it, but changed a pig for it." " And where did you get the pig?" "I gave a cow for it." "And the cow?" " I gave a horse for it." " And the horse?" " I gave a piece of silver as big as my head for that." " And the silver?" " Oh! I worked hard for that seven long years." " You have thriven well in the world hitherto," said the grinder; " now if you could find money in your pocket whenever you put your hand into it, your for-tune would be made." " Very true: but how is that to be managed?" " You must turn

grinder like me," said the other; "you only
want a grindstone; the rest will come of itself.
Here is one that is a little the worse for wear :
I would not ask more than the value of your
goose for it;—will you buy?" " How can you
ask such a question?" replied Hans; " I should
be the happiest man in the world, if I could
have money whenever I put my hand in my
pocket; what could I want more? there's the
goose!" " Now," said the grinder as he gave
him a common rough stone that lay by his side,
" this is a most capital stone; do but manage it
cleverly, and you can make an old nail cut
with it."

Hans took the stone and went off with a
light heart: his eyes sparkled for joy, and he
said to himself, " I must have been born in a
lucky hour; every thing that I want or wish
for comes to me of itself."

Meantime he began to be tired, for he had
been travelling ever since day-break; he was
hungry too, for he had given away his last
penny in his joy at getting the cow. At last
he could go no further, and the stone tired him
terribly; he dragged himself to the side of a

pond, that he might drink some water, and rest a while; so he laid the stone carefully by his side on the bank: but as he stooped down to drink, he forgot it, pushed it a little, and down it went plump into the pond. For a while he watched it sinking in the deep clear water, then sprang up for joy, and again fell upon his knees, and thanked Heaven with tears in his eyes for its kindness in taking away his only plague, the ugly heavy stone. " How happy am I ! " cried he : "no mortal was ever so lucky as I am." Then up he got with a light and merry heart, and walked on free from all his troubles, till he reached his mother's house.

THE TRAVELLING MUSICIANS,

OR THE WAITS OF BREMEN.

An honest farmer had once an ass, that had been a faithful servant to him a great many years, but was now growing old and every day more and more unfit for work. His master therefore was tired of keeping him and began

B 5

to think of putting an end to him; but the ass, who saw that some mischief was in the wind, took himself slyly off, and began his journey towards Bremen, "for there," thought he, "I may chance to be chosen town-musician."

After he had travelled a little way, he spied a dog lying by the road-side and panting as if he were very tired. "What makes you pant so, my friend?" said the ass. "Alas!" said the dog, "my master was going to knock me on the head, because I am old and weak, and can no longer make myself useful to him in hunting; so I ran away: but what can I do to earn my livelihood?" "Hark ye!" said the ass, "I am going to Bremen to turn musician: suppose you go with me, and try what you can do in the same way?" The dog said he was willing, and they jogged on together.

They had not gone far before they saw a cat sitting in the middle of the road and making a most rueful face. "Pray, my good lady," said the ass, "what's the matter with you? you look quite out of spirits!" "Ah me!" said the cat, "how can one be in good spirits when one's life is in danger? Because I am beginning to grow old, and had rather lie at my ease by the fire than run about the house after the mice, my mistress laid hold of me, and was going to drown me; and though I have been lucky enough to get away from her, I do not know what I am to live upon." "Oh!" said the ass, "by all means go with us to Bremen; you are a good night singer, and may make your fortune as one of the waits." The cat was pleased with the thought, and joined the party.

Soon afterwards, as they were passing by a farm-yard, they saw a cock perched upon a gate, and screaming out with all his might and main. "Bravo!" said the ass; "upon my word you make a famous noise; pray what is all this about?" "Why," said the cock, "I was just now saying that we should have fine weather for our washing-day, and yet my mistress and the cook don't thank me for my pains, but threaten to cut off my head tomorrow, and make broth of me for the guests that are coming on Sunday!" "Heaven forbid!" said the ass; "come with us, Master Chanticleer: it will be better, at any rate, than staying here to have your head cut off! Besides, who knows?

If we take care to sing in tune, we may get up a concert of our own: so come along with us." "With all my heart," said the cock: so they all four went on jollily together.

They could not, however, reach the town the first day; so when night came on, they went into a wood to sleep. The ass and the dog laid themselves down under a great tree, and the cat climbed up into the branches; while the cock, thinking that the higher he sat the safer he should be, flew up to the very top of the tree, and then, according to his custom, before he went to sleep, looked out on all sides of him to see that every thing was well. In doing this, he saw afar off something bright and shining; and calling to his companions said, "There must be a house no great way off, for I see a light." "If that be the case," said the ass, "we had better change our quarters, for our lodging is not the best in the world!" "Besides," added the dog, "I should not be the worse for a bone or two, or a bit of meat." So they walked off together towards the spot where Chanticleer had seen the light; and as they drew near, it became larger and brighter, till

they at last came close to a house in which a gang of robbers lived.

The ass, being the tallest of the company, marched up to the window and peeped in. " Well, Donkey," said Chanticleer, "what do you see?" "What do I see?" replied the ass, "why I see a table spread with all kinds of good things, and robbers sitting round it making merry." "That would be a noble lodging for us," said the cock. "Yes," said the ass, "if we could only get in:" so they consulted together how they should contrive to get the robbers out; and at last they hit upon a plan. The ass placed himself upright on his hind-legs, with his fore-feet resting against the window; the dog got upon his back; the cat scrambled up to the dog's shoulders, and the cock flew up and sat upon the cat's head. When all was ready, a signal was given, and they began their music. The ass brayed, the dog barked, the cat mewed, and the cock screamed: and then they all broke through the window at once, and came tumbling into the room, amongst the broken glass, with a most hideous clatter! The robbers, who had been not a little frightened by the opening concert, had now no doubt that some frightful hobgoblin had broken in upon them, and scampered away as fast as they could.

The coast once clear, our travellers soon sat down, and dispatched what the robbers had left, with as much eagerness as if they had not expected to eat again for a month. As soon as they had satisfied themselves, they put out the lights, and each once more sought out a resting-place to his own liking. The donkey laid himself down upon a heap of straw in the yard; the dog stretched himself upon a mat behind the door; the cat rolled herself up on the hearth before the warm ashes; and the cock perched upon a beam on the top of the house; and, as they were all rather tired with their journey, they soon fell asleep.

But about midnight, when the robbers saw from afar that the lights were out and that all seemed quiet, they began to think that they had been in too great a hurry to run away; and one of them, who was bolder than the rest,

went to see what was going on. Finding every
thing still, he marched into the kitchen, and
groped about till he found a match in order to
light a candle; and then, espying the glittering
fiery eyes of the cat, he mistook them for live
coals, and held the match to them to light it.
But the cat, not understanding this joke, sprung
at his face, and spit, and scratched at him.
This frightened him dreadfully, and away he
ran to the back door; but there the dog jumped
up and bit him in the leg; and as he was
crossing over the yard the ass kicked him; and
the cock, who had been awakened by the noise,
crowed with all his might. At this the robber
ran back as fast as he could to his comrades,
and told the captain "how a horrid witch
had got into the house, and had spit at him and
scratched his face with her long bony fingers;
how a man with a knife in his hand had hidden
himself behind the door, and stabbed him in
the leg; how a black monster stood in the yard
and struck him with a club; and how the devil
sat upon the top of the house and cried out,
' Throw the rascal up here !'" After this the
robbers never dared to go back to the house :

but the musicians were so pleased with their quarters, that they took up their abode there; and there they are, I dare say, at this very day.

THE GOLDEN BIRD.

A certain king had a beautiful garden, and in the garden stood a tree which bore golden apples. These apples were always counted, and about the time when they began to grow ripe it was found that every night one of them was gone. The king became very angry at this, and ordered the gardener to keep watch all night under the tree. The gardener set his eldest son to watch; but about twelve o'clock he fell asleep, and in the morning another of the apples was missing. Then the second son was ordered to watch; and at midnight he too felf asleep, and in the morning another apple was gone. Then the third son offered to keep watch; but the gardener at first would not let him, for fear some harm should come to him: however, at last he consented, and the young man laid himself under the tree to watch. As the clock struck twelve he heard a rustling noise in the air, and a bird came flying that was of pure gold; and as it was snapping at one of the apples with its beak, the gardener's son jumped up and shot an arrow at it. But the arrow did the bird no harm; only it dropped a golden feather from its tail, and then flew away. The golden feather was brought to the king in the morning, and all the council was called together. Every one agreed that it was worth more than all the wealth of the kingdom: but the king said, "One feather is of no use to me, I must have the whole bird."

Then the gardener's eldest son set out and thought to find the golden bird very easily; and when he had gone but a little way, he came to a wood, and by the side of the wood he saw a fox sitting; so he took his bow and made ready to shoot at it. Then the fox said, "Do not shoot me, for I will give you good coun- sel; I know what your business is, and that you want to find the golden bird. You will reach a village in the evening; and when you get there, you will see two inns opposite to

each other, one of which is very pleasant and
beautiful to look at: go not in there, but rest
for the night in the other, though it may appear to you to be very poor and mean." But
the son thought to himself, "What can such a
beast as this know about the matter?" So he
shot his arrow at the fox; but he missed it, and
it set up its tail above its back and ran into
the wood. Then he went his way, and in
the evening came to the village where the
two inns were; and in one of these were people singing, and dancing, and feasting; but
the other looked very dirty, and poor. " I
should be very silly," said he, " if I went to
that shabby house, and left this charming
place;" so he went into the smart house, and
ate and drank at his ease, and forgot the bird,
and his country too.

Time passed on; and as the eldest son did
not come back, and no tidings were heard of
him, the second son set out, and the same
thing happened to him. He met the fox, who
gave him the same good advice: but when he
came to the two inns, his eldest brother was
standing at the window where the merry-

making was, and called to him to come in ;
and he could not withstand the temptation,
but went in, and forgot the golden bird and
his country in the same manner.

Time passed on again, and the youngest son
too wished to set out into the wide world to
seek for the golden bird ; but his father would
not listen to it for a long while, for he was very
fond of his son, and was afraid that some ill
luck might happen to him also, and prevent
his coming back. However, at last it was
agreed he should go, for he would not rest at
home; and as he came to the wood, he met the
fox, and heard the same good counsel. But
he was thankful to the fox, and did not attempt
his life as his brothers had done; so the fox
said, " Sit upon my tail, and you will travel
faster." So he sat down, and the fox began to
run, and away they went over stock and stone
so quick that their hair whistled in the wind.

When they came to the village, the son followed the fox's counsel, and without looking
about him went to the shabby inn, and rested
there all night at his ease. In the morning
came the fox again, and met him as he was

beginning his journey, and said, "Go straight
forward till you come to a castle, before which
lie a whole troop of soldiers fast asleep and
snoring: take no notice of them, but go into the
castle and pass on and on till you come to a room,
where the golden bird sits in a wooden cage;
close by it stands a beautiful golden cage; but
do not try to take the bird out of the shabby
cage and put it into the handsome one, otherwise you will repent it." Then the fox stretched out his tail again, and the young man sat
himself down, and away they went over stock
and stone till their hair whistled in the wind.

Before the castle gate all was as the fox had
said: so the son went in and found the chamber
where the golden bird hung in a wooden cage,
and below stood the golden cage; and the three
golden apples that had been lost were lying
close by it. Then thought he to himself, "It
will be a very droll thing to bring away such
a fine bird in this shabby cage;" so he opened
the door and took hold of it and put it into
the golden cage. But the bird set up such a
loud scream that all the soldiers awoke, and
they took him prisoner and carried him before

the king. The next morning the court sat to judge him; and when all was heard, it sentenced him to die, unless he should bring the king the golden horse which could run as swiftly as the wind; and if he did this, he was to have the golden bird given him for his own.

So he set out once more on his journey, sighing, and in great despair, when on a sudden his good friend the fox met him, and said, "You see now what has happened on account of your not listening to my counsel. I will still, however, tell you how to find the golden horse, if you will do as I bid you. You must go straight on till you come to the castle where the horse stands in his stall: by his side will lie the groom fast asleep and snoring: take away the horse quietly, but be sure to put the old leathern saddle upon him, and not the golden one that is close by it." Then the son sat down on the fox's tail, and away they went over stock and stone till their hair whistled in the wind.

All went right, and the groom lay snoring with his hand upon the golden saddle. But when the son looked at the horse, he thought it a great pity to put the leathern saddle upon it. " I will give him the good one," said he; " I am sure he deserves it." As he took up the golden saddle, the groom awoke and cried out so loud, that all the guards ran in and took him prisoner, and in the morning he was again brought before the court to be judged, and was sentenced to die. But it was agreed, that, if he could bring thither the beautiful princess, he should live, and have the bird and the horse given him for his own.

Then he went his way again very sorrowful; but the old fox came and said, " Why did not you listen to me? If you had, you would have carried away both the bird and the horse; yet will I once more give you counsel. Go straight on, and in the evening you will arrive at a castle. At twelve o'clock at night the princess goes to the bathing-house: go up to her and give her a kiss, and she will let you lead her away; but take care you do not suffer her to go and take leave of her father and mother." Then the fox stretched out his tail, and so away they went over stock and stone till their hair whistled again.

As they came to the castle, all was as the fox had said, and at twelve o'clock the young man met the princess going to the bath, and gave her the kiss, and she agreed to run away with him, but begged with many tears that he would let her take leave of her father. At first he refused, but she wept still more and more, and fell at his feet, till at last he consented; but the moment she came to her father's house, the guards awoke and he was taken prisoner again.

Then he was brought before the king, and the king said, "You shall never have my daughter, unless in eight days you dig away the hill that stops the view from my window." Now this hill was so big that the whole world could not take it away: and when he had worked for seven days, and had done very little, the fox came and said, " Lie down and go to sleep; I will work for you." And in the morning he awoke and the hill was gone; so he went merrily to the king, and told him that now that it was removed he must give him the princess.

Then the king was obliged to keep his word, and away went the young man and the princess; and the fox came and said to him, "We will have all three, the princess, the horse, and the bird." "Ah!" said the young man, "that would be a great thing, but how can you contrive it?"

"If you will only listen," said the fox, "it can soon be done. When you come to the king, and he asks for the beautiful princess, you must say "Here she is!" Then he will be very joyful; and you will mount the golden horse that they are to give you, and put out your hand to take leave of them; but shake hands with the princess last. Then lift her quickly on to the horse behind you: clap your spurs to his side, and gallop away as fast as you can."

All went right: then the fox said, "When you come to the castle where the bird is, I will stay with the princess at the door, and you will ride in and speak to the king; and when he sees that it is the right horse, he will bring out the bird; but you must sit still, and say that you want to look at it, to see whether it is the true golden bird; and when you get it into your hand, ride away."

This, too, happened as the fox said; they

carried off the bird, the princess mounted again, and they rode on to a great wood. Then the fox came, and said, "Pray kill me, and cut off my head and my feet." But the young man refused to do it: so the fox said, "I will at any rate give you good counsel: beware of two things; ransom no one from the gallows, and sit down by the side of no river." Then away he went. "Well," thought the young man, "it is no hard matter to take that advice."

He rode on with the princess, till at last he came to the village where he had left his two brothers. And there he heard a great noise and uproar; and when he asked what was the matter, the people said, "Two men are going to be hanged." As he came nearer, he saw that the two men were his brothers, who had turned robbers; so he said, "Cannot they in any way be saved?" But the people said "No," unless he would bestow all his money upon the rascals and buy their liberty. Then he did not stay to think about the matter, but paid what was asked, and his brothers were given up, and went on with him towards their home.

And as they came to the wood where the fox first met them, it was so cool and pleasant that the two brothers said, " Let us sit down by the side of the river, and rest a while, to eat and drink." " Very well," said he, and forgot the fox's counsel, and sat down on the side of the river; and while he suspected nothing, they came behind, and threw him down the bank, and took the princess, the horse, and the bird, and went home to the king their master, and said, " All this have we won by our exertions." Then there was great rejoicing made; but the horse would not eat, the bird would not sing, and the princess wept.

The youngest son fell to the bottom of the river's bed: luckily it was nearly dry, but his bones were almost broken, and the bank was so steep that he could find no way to get out. Then the old fox came once more, and scolded him for not following his advice; otherwise no evil would have befallen him: " Yet," said he, " I cannot leave you here, so lay hold of my tail and hold fast." Then he pulled him out of the river, and said to him, as he got upon the bank, " Your brothers have set watch to

kill you, if they find you in the kingdom."
So he dressed himself as a poor man, and came
secretly to the king's court, and was scarcely
within the doors when the horse began to eat,
and the bird to sing, and the princess left off
weeping. He went straight to the king, and told
him all his brothers' roguery; and they were
seized and punished, and he had the princess
given to him again; and after the king's death
he was heir to his kingdom.

A long while after, he went to walk one day
in the wood, and the old fox met him, and besought him with tears in his eyes to kill him,
and cut off his head and feet. And at last he
did so, and in a moment the fox was changed
into a man, and turned out to be the brother
of the princess, who had been lost a great many
many years.

THE FISHERMAN AND HIS WIFE.

There was once a fisherman who lived with
his wife in a ditch, close by the sea-side. The
fisherman used to go out all day long a-fishing;

and one day, as he sat on the shore with his rod,
looking at the shining water and watching his
line, all on a sudden his float was dragged
away deep under the sea: and in drawing it
up he pulled a great fish out of the water.
The fish said to him, " Pray let me live: I
am not a real fish ; I am an enchanted prince,
put me in the water again, and let me go."
" Oh!" said the man, " you need not make so
many words about the matter; I wish to have
nothing to do with a fish that can talk; so swim
away as soon as you please." Then he put
him back into the water, and the fish darted
straight down to the bottom, and left a long
streak of blood behind him.

When the fisherman went home to his wife
in the ditch, he told her how he had caught a
great fish, and how it had told him it was an
enchanted prince, and that on hearing it speak
he had let it go again. " Did you not ask it
for any thing?" said the wife. " No," said the
man, " what should I ask for?" " Ah!" said
the wife, " we live very wretchedly here in this
nasty stinking ditch; do go back, and tell the
fish we want a little cottage."

The fisherman did not much like the business: however, he went to the sea, and when
he came there the water looked all yellow and
green. And he stood at the water's edge, and
said,

" O man of the sea!
Come listen to me,
For Alice my wife,
The plague of my life,
Hath sent me to beg a boon of thee ! "

Then the fish came swimming to him, and
said, " Well, what does she want?" " Ah!"
answered the fisherman, " my wife says that
when I had caught you, I ought to have asked
you for something before I let you go again; she
does not like living any longer in the ditch,
and wants a little cottage." " Go home, then,"
said the fish, " she is in the cottage already."
So the man went home, and saw his wife standing at the door of a cottage. " Come in, come
in," said she; " is not this much better than
the ditch?" And there was a parlour, and a
bed-chamber, and a kitchen; and behind the
cottage there was a little garden with all sorts
of flowers and fruits, and a court-yard full of

ducks and chickens. "Ah!" said the fisherman, "how happily we shall live!" "We will try to do so at least," said his wife.

Every thing went right for a week or two, and then Dame Alice said, "Husband, there is not room enough in this cottage, the court-yard and garden are a great deal too small; I should like to have a large stone castle to live in; so go to the fish again, and tell him to give us a castle." "Wife," said the fisherman, "I don't like to go to him again, for perhaps he will be angry; we ought to be content with the cottage." "Nonsense!" said the wife; "he will do it very willingly; go along, and try."

The fisherman went; but his heart was very heavy: and when he came to the sea, it looked blue and gloomy, though it was quite calm, and he went close to it, and said,

> "O man of the sea!
> Come listen to me,
> For Alice my wife,
> The plague of my life,
> Hath sent me to beg a boon of thee!"

"Well, what does she want now?" said the fish. "Ah!" said the man very sorrowfully,

" my wife wants to live in a stone castle."
" Go home then," said the fish, " she is standing at the door of it already."   So away went
the fisherman, and found his wife standing before a great castle.   " See," said she, " is not
this grand?"   With that they went into the
castle together, and found a great many servants there, and the rooms all richly furnished
and full of golden chairs and tables; and behind the castle was a garden, and a wood half
a mile long, full of sheep, and goats, and hares,
and deer; and in the court-yard were stables
and cow-houses.   " Well!" said the man,
" now will we live contented and happy in
this beautiful castle for the rest of our lives."
" Perhaps we may," said the wife; " but let
us consider and sleep upon it before we make
up our minds:" so they went to bed.

The next morning, when Dame Alice awoke,
it was broad day-light, and she jogged the
fisherman with her elbow, and said, " Get up,
husband, and bestir yourself, for we must be
king of all the land."   " Wife, wife," said the
man, " why should we wish to be king?   I
will not be king."   " Then I will," said Alice.

" But, wife," answered the fisherman, " how can you be king? the fish cannot make you a king." " Husband," said she, " say no more about it, but go and try; I will be king!" So the man went away, quite sorrowful to think that his wife should want to be king. The sea looked a dark grey colour, and was covered with foam as he cried out,

> " O man of the sea !
> Come listen to me,
> For Alice my wife,
> The plague of my life,
> Hath sent me to beg a boon of thee ! "

" Well, what would she have now?" said the fish. " Alas!" said the man, " my wife wants to be king." " Go home," said the fish; " she is king already."

Then the fisherman went home; and as he came close to the palace, he saw a troop of soldiers, and heard the sound of drums and trumpets; and when he entered in, he saw his wife sitting on a high throne of gold and diamonds, with a golden crown upon her head; and on each side of her stood six beautiful maidens, each a head taller than the other.

" Well, wife," said the fisherman, " are you king?" " Yes," said she, "I am king." And when he had looked at her for a long time, he said, " Ah, wife ! what a fine thing it is to be king ! now we shall never have any thing more to wish for." " I don't know how that may be," said she; " never is a long time. I am king, 'tis true, but I begin to be tired of it, and I think I should like to be emperor." " Alas, wife ! why should you wish to be emperor?" said the fisherman. " Husband," said she, " go to the fish; I say I will be emperor." " Ah, wife!" replied the fisherman, " the fish cannot make an emperor, and I should not like to ask for such a thing." " I am king," said Alice, " and you are my slave, so go directly !" So the fisherman was obliged to go; and he muttered as he went along, " This will come to no good, it is too much to ask, the fish will be tired at last, and then we shall repent of what we have done." He soon arrived at the sea, and the water was quite black and muddy, and a mighty whirlwind blew over it ; but he went to the shore, and said,

c 5

" O man of the sea !
  Come listen to me,
  For Alice my wife,
  The plague of my life,
Hath sent me to beg a boon of thee !"

" What would she have now?" said the fish.
" Ah !" said the fisherman, "she wants to be
emperor." " Go home," said the fish; "she
is emperor already."

So he went home again; and as he came
near he saw his wife sitting on a very lofty
throne made of solid gold, with a great crown
on her head full two yards high, and on each
side of her stood her guards and attendants in a
row, each one smaller than the other, from the
tallest giant down to a little dwarf no bigger
than my finger. And before her stood princes,
and dukes, and earls: and the fisherman went
up to her and said, "Wife, are you emperor?"
" Yes," said she, " I am emperor." " Ah !"
said the man as he gazed upon her, "what a
fine thing it is to be emperor !" "Husband,"
said she, " why should we stay at being emperor? I will be pope next." " O wife, wife !"

said he, "how can you be pope? there is but one pope at a time in Christendom." "Husband," said she, "I will be pope this very day." "But," replied the husband, "the fish cannot make you pope." "What nonsense!" said she, "if he can make an emperor, he can make a pope; go and try him." So the fisherman went. But when he came to the shore the wind was raging, and the sea was tossed up and down like boiling water, and the ships were in the greatest distress and danced upon the waves most fearfully; in the middle of the sky there was a little blue, but towards the south it was all red as if a dreadful storm was rising. At this the fisherman was terribly frightened and trembled, so that his knees knocked together: but he went to the shore and said,

"O man of the sea!
Come listen to me,
For Alice my wife,
The plague of my life,
Hath sent me to beg a boon of thee!"

"What does she want now?" said the fish. "Ah!" said the fisherman, "my wife wants to be pope." "Go home," said the fish, "she is pope already."

Then the fisherman went home, and found his wife sitting on a throne that was two miles high; and she had three great crowns on her head, and around stood all the pomp and power of the church; and on each side were two rows of burning lights, of all sizes, the greatest as large as the highest and biggest tower in the world, and the least no larger than a small rush-light. "Wife," said the fisherman as he look-ed at all this grandeur, "are you pope?" "Yes," said she, "I am pope." "Well, wife," replied he, "it is a grand thing to be pope; and now you must be content, for you can be nothing greater." "I will consider of that," said the wife. Then they went to bed: but Dame Alice could not sleep all night for think-ing what she should be next. At last morn-ing came, and the sun rose. "Ha!" thought she as she looked at it through the window, "cannot I prevent the sun rising?" At this she was very angry, and wakened her hus-band, and said, "Husband, go to the fish and tell him I want to be lord of the sun and moon." The fisherman was half asleep, but the thought frightened him so much, that he started and fell out of bed. " Alas, wife !" said he, "cannot you be content to be pope?" "No," said she, "I am very uneasy, and cannot bear to see the sun and moon rise without my leave. Go to the fish directly."

Then the man went trembling for fear; and as he was going down to the shore a dreadful storm arose, so that the trees and the rocks shook; and the heavens became black, and the lightning played, and the thunder rolled; and you might have seen in the sea great black waves like mountains with a white crown of foam upon them; and the fisherman said,

" O man of the sea !
　Come listen to me,
　For Alice my wife,
　The plague of my life,
Hath sent me to beg a boon of thee ! "

" What does she want now ? " said the fish. " Ah !" said he, "she wants to be lord of the sun and moon." "Go home," said the fish, "to your ditch again!" And there they live to this very day.

———

THE TOM-TIT AND THE BEAR.

ONE summer day, as the wolf and the bear were walking together in a wood, they heard a bird singing most delightfully. "Brother," said the bear, "what can that bird be that is singing so sweetly?" "O!" said the wolf "that is his majesty the king of the birds; we must take care to show him all possible respect." (Now I should tell you that this bird was after all no other than the tom-tit.) "If that is the case," said the bear, "I should like to see the royal palace; so pray come along and show it to me." "Gently, my friend," said the wolf, "we cannot see it just yet, we must wait till the queen comes home."

Soon afterwards the queen came with food in her beak, and she and the king began to feed their young ones. " Now for it! " said the bear; and was about to follow them, to see what was to be seen. " Stop a little, master Bruin," said the wolf, " we must wait now till their majesties are gone again." So they marked the hole where they had seen the nest, and went away. But the bear, being very eager to see the royal palace, soon came back again, and peeping into the nest, saw five or six young birds lying at the bottom of it. " What nonsense!" said Bruin, "this is not a royal palace: I never saw such a filthy place in my life; and you are no royal children, you little base-born brats! " As soon as the young tom-tits heard this they were very angry, and screamed out " We are not base-born, you stupid bear! our father and mother are honest good sort of people: and depend upon it you shall suffer for your insolence!" At this the wolf and the bear grew frightened, and ran away to their dens. But the young tom-tits kept crying and screaming; and when their father and mother came home and offered them food, they all said, " We will not touch a bit; no, not the leg of a fly, though we should die of hunger, till that rascal Bruin has been punished for calling us base-born brats." " Make yourselves easy, my darlings," said the old king, " you may be sure he shall meet with his deserts."

So he went out and stood before the bear's den, and cried out with a loud voice, " Bruin the bear ! thou hast shamefully insulted our lawful children: we therefore hereby declare bloody and cruel war against thee and thine, which shall never cease until thou hast been punished as thou so richly deservest."   Now when the bear heard this, he called together the ox, the ass, the stag, and all the beasts of the earth, in order to consult about the means of his defence.   And the tom-tit also enlisted on his side all the birds of the air, both great and small, and a very large army of hornets, gnats, bees, and flies, and other insects.

As the time approached when the war was to begin, the tom-tit sent out spies to see who was the commander-in-chief of the enemy's forces; and the gnat, who was by far the cleverest spy of them all, flew backwards and forwards in the wood where the enemy's troops were, and at last hid himself under a leaf on a tree, close by which the orders of the day were given out. And the bear, who was standing so near the tree that the gnat could hear all he said, called to the fox and said, "Reynard, you are the cleverest of all the beasts; therefore you shall be our general and lead us to battle: but we must first agree upon some signal, by which we may know what you want us to do." "Behold," said the fox, "I have a fine, long, bushy tail, which is very like a plume of red feathers, and gives me a very warlike air: now remember, when you see me raise up my tail, you may be sure that the battle is won, and you have then nothing to do but to rush down upon the enemy with all your force. On the other hand, if I drop my tail, the day is lost, and you must run away as fast as you can." Now when the gnat had heard all this, she flew back to the tom-tit, and told him every thing that had passed.

At length the day came when the battle was to be fought; and as soon as it was light, be-hold! the army of beasts came rushing forward with such a fearful sound that the earth shook. And his majesty the tom-tit, with his troops,

came flying along in warlike array, flapping
and fluttering, and beating the air, so that it
was quite frightful to hear; and both armies set
themselves in order of battle upon the field.
Now the tom-tit gave orders to a troop of hornets that at the first onset they should march
straight towards Captain Reynard, and fixing
themselves about his tail, should sting him with
all their might and main. The hornets did as
they were told: and when Reynard felt the first
sting, he started aside and shook one of his
legs, but still held up his tail with wonderful
bravery; at the second sting he was forced to
drop his tail for a moment; but when the third
hornet had fixed itself, he could bear it no
longer, but clapped his tail b tween his legs
and scampered away as fast as he could. As
soon as the beasts saw this, they thought of
course all was lost, and scoured across the
country in the greatest dismay, leaving the
birds masters of the field.

And now the king and queen flew back in
triumph to their children, and s id, "Now, children, eat, drink, and be merry, for the victory
is ours!" But the young birds said, "No:

not till Bruin has humbly begged our pardon for calling us base-born." So the king flew back to the bear's den, and cried out, " Thou villain bear! come forthwith to my abode, and humbly beseech my children to forgive thee the insult thou hast offered them; for, if thou wilt not do this, every bone in thy wretched body shall be broken to pieces." Then the bear was forced to crawl out of his den very sulkily, and do what the king bade him: and after that the young birds sat down together, and ate and drank and made merry till midnight.

TWELVE DANCING PRINCESSES.

There was a king who had twelve beautiful daughters. They slept in twelve beds all in one room; and when they went to bed, the doors were shut and locked up; but every morning their shoes were found to be quite worn through, as if they had been danced in all night; and yet nobody could find out how it happened, or where they had been.

Then the king made it known to all the land, that if any person could discover the secret, and find out where it was that the princesses danced in the night, he should have the one he liked best for his wife, and should be king after his death; but whoever tried and did not succeed, after three days and nights, should be put to death.

A king's son soon came. He was well entertained, and in the evening was taken to the chamber next to the one where the princesses lay in their twelve beds. There he was to sit and watch where they went to dance; and in order that nothing might pass without his hearing it, the door of his chamber was left open. But the king's son soon fell asleep; and when he awoke in the morning he found that the princesses had all been dancing, for the soles of their shoes were full of holes. The same thing happened the second and third night: so the king ordered his head to be cut off. After him came several others; but they had all the same luck, and all lost their lives in the same manner.

Now it chanced that an old soldier, who had been wounded in battle and could fight no longer, passed through the country where this king reigned: and as he was travelling through a wood, he met an old woman, who asked him where he was going. " I hardly know where I am going, or what I had better do," said the soldier; " but I think I should like very well to find out where it is that the princesses dance, and then in time I might be a king." " Well," said the old dame, " that is no very hard task: only take care not to drink any of the wine which one of the princesses will bring to you in the evening; and as soon as she leaves you pretend to be fast asleep."

Then she gave him a cloak, and said, " As soon as you put that on you will become invisible, and you will then be able to follow the princesses wherever they go." When the soldier heard all this good counsel, he determined to try his luck: so he went to the king, and said he was willing to undertake the task.

He was as well received as the others had

been, and the king ordered fine royal robes to
be given him; and when the evening came, he
was led to the outer chamber. Just as he was
going to lie down, the eldest of the princesses
brought him a cup of wine; but the soldier
threw it all away secretly, taking care not to
drink a drop. Then he laid himself down on
his bed, and in a little while began to snore
very loud as if he was fast asleep. When the
twelve princesses heard this they laughed heartily; and the eldest said, "This fellow too might
have done a wiser thing than lose his life in
this way!" Then they rose up and opened
their drawers and boxes, and took out all their
fine clothes, and dressed themselves at the glass,
and skipped about as if they were eager to begin dancing. But the youngest said, " I don't
know how it is, while you are so happy I feel
very uneasy; I am sure some mischance will
befall us." "You simpleton," said the eldest,
" you are always afraid; have you forgotten
how many kings' sons have already watched us
in vain? And as for this soldier, even if I had
not given him his sleeping draught, he would
have slept soundly enough."

When they were all ready, they went and looked at the soldier: but he snored on, and did not stir hand or foot: so they thought they were quite safe; and the eldest went up to her own bed and clapped her hands, and the bed sank into the floor and a trap-door flew open. The soldier saw them going down through the trap-door one after another, the eldest leading the way; and thinking he had no time to lose, he jumped up, put on the cloak which the old woman had given him, and followed them; but in the middle of the stairs he trod on the gown of the youngest princess, and she cried out to her sisters, " All is not right; some one took hold of my gown." " You silly creature ! " said the eldest, " it is nothing but a nail in the wall." Then down they all went, and at the bottom they found themselves in a most delightful grove of trees; and the leaves were all of silver, and glittered and sparkled beautifully. The soldier wished to take away some token of the place; so he broke off a little branch, and there came a loud noise from the tree. Then the youngest daughter said again, " I am sure all is not right—did not

you hear that noise? That never happened
before." But the eldest said, " It is only the
princes, who are shouting for joy at our ap-
proach."

Then they came to another grove of trees,
where all the leaves were of gold; and afterwards to a third, where the leaves were all
glittering diamonds. And the soldier broke a
branch from each; and every time there was a
loud noise, which made the youngest sister
tremble with fear; but the eldest still said,
it was only the princes, who were crying for
joy. So they went on till they came to a
great lake; and at the side of the lake there
lay twelve little boats with twelve handsome
princes in them, who seemed to be waiting
there for the princesses.

One of the princesses went into each boat,
and the soldier stepped into the same boat with
the youngest. As they were rowing over the
lake, the prince who was in the boat with the
youngest princess and the soldier said, " I do
not know why it is, but though I am rowing
with all my might, we do not get on so fast as
usual, and I am quite tired: the boat seems

very heavy to-day." " It is only the heat of the weather," said the princess; " I feel it very warm too."

On the other side of the lake stood a fine il-luminated castle, from which came the merry music of horns and trumpets. There they all landed, and went into the castle, and each prince danced with his princess; and the sol-dier, who was all the time invisible, danced with them too; and when any of the princesses had a cup of wine set by her, he drank it all up, so that when she put the cup to her mouth it was empty. At this, too, the youngest sister was terribly frightened, but the eldest always silenced her. They danced on till three o'clock in the morning, and then all their shoes were worn out, so that they were obliged to leave off. The princes rowed them back again over the lake; (but this time the soldier placed him-self in the boat with the eldest princess;) and on the opposite shore they took leave of each other, the princesses promising to come again the next night.

When they came to the stairs, the soldier ran on before the princesses, and laid himself

D

down; and as the twelve sisters slowly came
up very much tired, they heard him snoring in
his bed; so they said, " Now all is quite safe:"
then they undressed themselves, put away their
fine clothes, pulled off their shoes, and went to
bed. In the morning the soldier said nothing
about what had happened, but determined to
see more of this strange adventure, and went
again the second and third night; and every
thing happened just as before; the princesses
danced each time till their shoes were worn to
pieces, and then returned home. However,
on the third night the soldier carried away one
of the golden cups as a token of where he had
been.

As soon as the time came when he was to
declare the secret, he was taken before the
king with the three branches and the golden
cup; and the twelve princesses stood listening
behind the door to hear what he would say.
And when the king asked him " Where do my
twelve daughters dance at night?" he answered,
"With twelve princes in a castle under ground."
And then he told the king all that had happened,
and showed him the three branches and the

golden cup which he had brought with him.
Then the king called for the princesses, and
asked them whether what the soldier said was
true: and when they saw that they were disco-
vered, and that it was of no use to deny what
had happened, they confessed it all. And the
king asked the soldier which of them he would
choose for his wife; and he answered, " I am
not very young, so I will have the eldest."—
And they were married that very day, and the
soldier was chosen to be the king's heir.

ROSE-BUD.

Once upon a time there lived a king and
queen who had no children; and this they la-
mented very much. But one day as the queen
was walking by the side of the river, a little
fish lifted its head out of the water, and said,
" Your wish shall be fulfilled, and you shall
soon have a daughter." What the little fish

had foretold soon came to pass; and the queen had a little girl that was so very beautiful that the king could not cease looking on it for joy, and determined to hold a great feast. So he invited not only his relations, friends, and neighbours, but also all the fairies, that they might be kind and good to his little daughter. Now there were thirteen fairies in his kingdom, and he had only twelve golden dishes for them to eat out of, so that he was obliged to leave one of the fairies without an invitation. The rest came, and after the feast was over they gave all their best gifts to the little princess: one gave her virtue, another beauty, another riches, and so on, till she had all that was excellent in the world. When eleven had done blessing her, the thirteenth, who had not been invited, and was very angry on that account, came in, and determined to take her revenge. So she cried out, " The king's daughter shall in her fifteenth year be wounded by a spindle, and fall down dead." Then the twelfth, who had not yet given her gift, came forward and said, that the bad wish must be fulfilled, but that she could soften it, and that the king's daughter should not die, but fall asleep for a hundred years.

But the king hoped to save his dear child from the threatened evil, and ordered that all the spindles in the kingdom should be bought up and destroyed. All the fairies' gifts were in the mean time fulfilled; for the princess was so beautiful, and well-behaved, and amiable, and wise, that every one who knew her loved her. Now it happened that on the very day she was fifteen years old the king and queen were not at home, and she was left alone in the palace. So she roved about by herself, and looked at all the rooms and chambers, till at last she came to an old tower, to which there was a narrow staircase ending with a little door. In the door there was a golden key, and when she turned it the door sprang open, and there sat an old lady spinning away very busily. "Why, how now, good mother," said the princess, "what are you doing there?" "Spinning," said the old lady, and nodded her head. "How prettily that little thing turns round!" said the princess, and took the spindle and be-

gan to spin. But scarcely had she touched it,
before the prophecy was fulfilled, and she fell
down lifeless on the ground.

However, she was not dead, but had only
fallen into a deep sleep; and the king and the
queen, who just then came home, and all their
court, fell asleep too; and the horses slept in
the stables, and the dogs in the court, the pigeons on the house-top, and the flies on the
walls. Even the fire on the hearth left off
blazing, and went to sleep; and the meat that
was roasting stood still; and the cook, who
was at that moment pulling the kitchen-boy
by the hair to give him a box on the ear for
something he had done amiss, let him go, and
both fell asleep; and so every thing stood still,
and slept soundly.

A large hedge of thorns soon grew round
the palace, and every year it became higher
and thicker, till at last the whole palace was
surrounded and hid, so that not even the roof
or the chimneys could be seen. But there went
a report through all the land of the beautiful
sleeping Rose-Bud (for so was the king's
daughter called); so that from time to time

several kings' sons came, and tried to break through the thicket into the palace. This they could never do; for the thorns and bushes laid hold of them as it were with hands, and there they stuck fast and died miserably.

After many many years there came a king's son into that land, and an old man told him the story of the thicket of thorns, and how a beautiful palace stood behind it, in which was a wondrous princess, called Rose-Bud, asleep with all her court. He told too, how he had heard from his grandfather that many many princes had come, and had tried to break through the thicket, but had stuck fast and died. Then the young prince said, " All this shall not frighten me, I will go and see Rose-Bud." The old man tried to dissuade him, but he persisted in going.

Now that very day were the hundred years completed; and as the prince came to the thicket, he saw nothing but beautiful flowering shrubs, through which he passed with ease, and they closed after him as firm as ever. Then he came at last to the palace, and there in the court lay the dogs asleep, and the horses

in the stables, and on the roof sat the pigeons
fast asleep with their heads under their wings;
and when he came into the palace, the flies
slept on the walls, and the cook in the kitchen
was still holding up her hand as if she would
beat the boy, and the maid sat with a black
fowl in her hand ready to be plucked.

Then he went on still further, and all was
so still that he could hear every breath he
drew; till at last he came to the old tower
and opened the door of the little room in which
Rose-Bud was, and there she lay fast asleep,
and looked so beautiful that he could not take
his eyes off, and he stooped down and gave
her a kiss. But the moment he kissed her she
opened her eyes and awoke, and smiled upon
him. Then they went out together, and presently the king and queen also awoke, and all
the court, and they gazed on each other with
great wonder. And the horses got up and
shook themselves, and the dogs jumped about
and barked; the pigeons took their heads from
under their wings, and looked about and flew
into the fields; the flies on the walls buzzed
away; the fire in the kitchen blazed up and

cooked the dinner, and the roast meat turned round again; the cook gave the boy the box on his ear so that he cried out, and the maid went on plucking the fowl. And then was the wedding of the prince and Rose-Bud celebrated, and they lived happily together all their lives long.

TOM THUMB.

There was once a poor woodman sitting by the fire in his cottage, and his wife sat by his side spinning. "How lonely it is," said he, "for you and me to sit here by ourselves, without any children to play about and amuse us, while other people seem so happy and merry with their children!" "What you say is very true," said the wife, sighing and turning round her wheel, "how happy should I be if I had but one child! and if it were ever so small, nay, if it were no bigger than my thumb, I should be very happy, and love it dearly."

Now it came to pass that this good woman's
wish was fulfilled just as she desired; for, some
time afterwards, she had a little boy who was
quite healthy and strong, but not much bigger
than my thumb.   So they said, " Well, we
cannot say we have not got what we wished
for, and, little as he is, we will love him dearly;" and they called him Tom Thumb.

They gave him plenty of food, yet he never
grew bigger, but remained just the same size
as when he was born; still his eyes were sharp
and sparkling, and he soon showed himself to
be a clever little fellow, who always knew well
what he was about.   One day, as the woodman was getting ready to go into the wood to
cut fuel, he said, " I wish I had some one to
bring the cart after me, for I want to make
haste."   " O father!" cried Tom, " I will
take care of that; the cart shall be in the wood
by the time you want it."   Then the woodman laughed, and said, " How can that be?
you cannot reach up to the horse's bridle."
" Never mind that, father," said Tom: " if my
mother will only harness the horse, I will get

into his ear and tell him which way to go." " Well," said the father, " we will try for once."

When the time came, the mother harnessed the horse to the cart, and put Tom into his ear; and as he sat there, the little man told the beast how to go, crying out, " Go on," and " Stop," as he wanted : so the horse went on just as if the woodman had driven it himself into the wood. It happened that, as the horse was going a little too fast, and Tom was calling out " Gently! gently!" two strangers came up. " What an odd thing that is!" said one, " there is a cart going along, and I hear a carter talking to the horse, but can see no one." " That is strange," said the other; " let us follow the cart and see where it goes." So they went on into the wood, till at last they came to the place where the woodman was. Then Tom Thumb, seeing his father, cried out, " See, father, here I am, with the cart, all right and safe; now take me down." So his father took hold of the horse with one hand, and with the other took his son out of the ear; then he put him down upon a straw, where he sat as merry as you please. The two strangers were all this time looking on, and did not know what to say for wonder. At last one took the other aside and said, "That little urchin will make our fortune if we can get him and carry him about from town to town as a show: we must buy him." So they went to the woodman and asked him what he would take for the little man: "He will be better off," said they, "with us than with you." "I won't sell him at all," said the father; "my own flesh and blood is dearer to me than all the silver and gold in the world." But Tom, hearing of the bargain they wanted to make, crept up his father's coat to his shoulder, and whispered in his ear, "Take the money, father, and let them have me; I'll soon come back to you."

So the woodman at last agreed to sell Tom to the strangers for a large piece of gold. "Where do you like to sit?" said one of them. "Oh! put me on the rim of your hat, that will be a nice gallery for me; I can walk about there, and see the country as we go along." So they did as he wished; and when Tom had

taken leave of his father, they took him away
with them. They journeyed on till it began
to be dusky, and then the little man said, " Let
me get down, I'm tired." So the man took
off his hat, and set him down on a clod of earth
in a ploughed field by the side of the road.
But Tom ran about amongst the furrows, and
at last slipt into an old mouse-hole. " Good
night, masters," said he, " I'm off! mind and
look sharp after me the next time." They ran
directly to the place, and poked the ends of
their sticks into the mouse-hole, but all in vain;
Tom only crawled further and further in, and
at last it became quite dark, so that they were
obliged to go their way without their prize, as
sulky as you please.

When Tom found they were gone, he came
out of his hiding-place. " What dangerous
walking it is," said he, "in this ploughed field!
If I were to fall from one of these great clods,
I should certainly break my neck." At last,
by good luck, he found a large empty snail-
shell. " This is lucky," said he, " I can sleep
here very well," and in he crept. Just as he
was falling asleep he heard two men passing,

and one said to the other, " How shall we manage to steal that rich parson's silver and gold?"
" I'll tell you," cried Tom. " What noise was
that?" said the thief, frightened, " I am sure I
heard some one speak." They stood still listening, and Tom said, " Take me with you, and
I'll soon show you how to get the parson's
money." " But where are you?" said they.
" Look about on the ground," answered he,
" and listen where the sound comes from."
At last the thieves found him out, and lifted
him up in their hands. " You little urchin !"
said they, " what can you do for us?" " Why
I can get between the iron window-bars of the
parson's house, and throw you out whatever
you want." " That's a good thought," said
the thieves, " come along, we shall see what
you can do."

When they came to the parson's house,
Tom slipt through the window-bars into the
room, and then called out as loud as he could
bawl, " Will you have all that is here?" At
this the thieves were frightened, and said,
" Softly, softly! Speak low, that you may not
awaken any body." But Tom pretended not

to understand them, and bawled out again,
" How much will you have? Shall I throw it
all out?" Now the cook lay in the next room,
and hearing a noise she raised herself in her
bed and listened. Meantime the thieves were
frightened, and ran off to a little distance; but
at last they plucked up courage, and said,
" The little urchin is only trying to make fools
of us." So they came back and whispered
softly to him, saying, " Now let us have no
more of your jokes, but throw out some of the
money." Then Tom called out as loud as he
could, " Very well: hold your hands, here it
comes." The cook heard this quite plain, so
she sprang out of bed and ran to open the door.
The thieves ran off as if a wolf was at their
tails; and the maid, having groped about and
found nothing, went away for a light. By the
time she returned, Tom had slipt off into the
barn; and when the cook had looked about
and searched every hole and corner, and found
nobody, she went to bed, thinking she must
have been dreaming with her eyes open. The
little man crawled about in the hay-loft, and at
last found a glorious place to finish his night's

rest in; so he laid himself down, meaning to sleep till day-light, and then find his way home to his father and mother. But, alas! how cruelly was he disappointed! what crosses and sorrows happen in this world! The cook got up early before day-break to feed the cows: she went straight to the hay-loft, and carried away a large bundle of hay with the little man in the middle of it fast asleep. He still, however, slept on, and did not awake till he found himself in the mouth of the cow, who had taken him up with a mouthful of hay: "Good lack-a-day!" said he, "how did I manage to tumble into the mill?" But he soon found out where he really was, and was obliged to have all his wits about him in order that he might not get between the cow's teeth, and so be crushed to death. At last down he went into her stomach. "It is rather dark here," said he; "they forgot to build windows in this room to let the sun in: a candle would be no bad thing."

Though he made the best of his bad luck, he did not like his quarters at all; and the worst of it was, that more and more hay was always coming down, and the space in which he was, became smaller and smaller. At last he cried out as loud as he could, "Don't bring me any more hay! Don't bring me any more hay!" The maid happened to be just then milking the cow, and hearing some one speak and seeing nobody, and yet being quite sure it was the same voice that she had heard in the night, she was so frightened that she fell off her stool and overset the milk-pail. She ran off as fast as she could to her master the parson, and said, "Sir, sir, the cow is talking!" But the parson said, "Woman, thou art surely mad!" However, he went with her into the cow-house to see what was the matter.— Scarcely had they set their foot on the threshold, when Tom called out, "Don't bring me any more hay!" Then the parson himself was frightened; and thinking the cow was surely bewitched, ordered that she should be killed directly. So the cow was killed, and the stomach, in which Tom lay, was thrown out upon a dunghill.

Tom soon set himself to work to get out, which was not a very easy task; but at last,

just as he had made room to get his head out,
a new misfortune befell him : a hungry wolf
sprang out, and swallowed the whole stomach
with Tom in it at a single gulp, and ran away·
Tom, however, was not disheartened; and,
thinking the wolf would not dislike having
some chat with him as he was going along,
he called out, "My good friend, I can show
you a famous treat." "Where's that?" said
the wolf. " In such and such a house," said
Tom, describing his father's house, "you
can crawl through the drain into the kitchen,
and there you will find cakes, ham, beef, and
every thing your heart can desire." The wolf
did not want to be asked twice; so that very
night he went to the house and crawled through
the drain into the kitchen, and ate and drank
there to his heart's content. As soon as he
was satisfied, he wanted to get away, but he
had eaten so much that he could not get out
the same way that he came in. This was just
what Tom had reckoned upon; and he now
began to set up a great shout, making all the
noise he could. "Will you be quiet?" said
the wolf: "you'll awaken every body in the

house." " What's that to me?" said the
little man: "you have had your frolic, now
I've a mind to be merry myself;" and he began again singing and shouting as loud as he
could.

The woodman and his wife, being awakened
by the noise, peeped through a crack in the
door; but when they saw that the wolf was
there, you may well suppose that they were
terribly frightened; and the woodman ran
for his axe, and gave his wife a scythe.—
" Now do you stay behind," said the woodman; "and when I have knocked him on the
head, do you rip up his belly for him with
the scythe." Tom heard all this, and said,
" Father, father! I am here, the wolf has
swallowed me:" and his father said, " Heaven
be praised! we have found our dear child
again;" and he told his wife not to use the
scythe, for fear she should hurt him. Then he
aimed a great blow, and struck the wolf on
the head, and killed him on the spot; and
when he was dead they cut open his body and
set Tommy free. " Ah!" said the father,
" what fears we have had for you!" " Yes,

father," answered he, "I have travelled all over the world, since we parted, in one way or other; and now I am very glad to get fresh air again." "Why, where have you been?" said his father. "I have been in a mouse-hole, in a snail-shell, down a cow's throat, and in the wolf's belly; and yet here I am again safe and sound." "Well," said they, "we will not sell you again for all the riches in the world." So they hugged and kissed their dear little son, and gave him plenty to eat and drink, and fetched new clothes for him, for his old ones were quite spoiled on his journey.

THE GRATEFUL BEASTS.

A CERTAIN man, who had lost almost all his money, resolved to set off with the little that was left him, and travel into the wide world. Then the first place he came to was a village, where the young people were running about crying and shouting. "What is the matter?"

asked he. " See here," answered they, "we have got a mouse that we make dance to please us. Do look at him: what a droll sight it is! how he jumps about!" But the man pitied the poor little thing, and said, "Let the mouse go, and I will give you money. So he gave them some, and took the mouse and let it run; and it soon jumped into a hole that was close by, and was out of their reach.

Then he travelled on and came to another village, and there the children had got an ass that they made stand on its hind legs, and tumble and cut capers, at which they laughed and shouted, and gave the poor beast no rest. So the good man gave them some of his money to let the poor creature go away in peace.

At the next village he came to, the young people had found a bear that had been taught to dance, and they were plaguing the poor thing sadly. Then he gave them too some money to let the beast go, and the bear was very glad to get on his four feet, and seemed quite at his ease and happy again.

But now he found that he had given away all the money he had in the world, and had not a

shilling in his pocket. Then said he to himself,
" The king has heaps of gold in his treasury
that he never uses; I cannot die of hunger, I
hope I shall be forgiven, if I borrow a little,
and when I get rich again I will repay it all."

So he managed to get into the treasury, and
took a very little money; but as he came out
the king's guards saw him, and said he was a
thief, and took him to the judge, and he was
sentenced to be thrown into the water in a
box. The lid of the box was full of holes to
let in air, and a jug of water and a loaf of
bread were given him.

Whilst he was swimming along in the water very sorrowfully, he heard something nib-
bling and biting at the lock; and all of a sudden it fell off, the lid flew open, and there stood
his old friend the little mouse, who had done
him this service. And then came the ass and
the bear, and pulled the box ashore; and all
helped him because he had been kind to them.

But now they did not know what to do next,
and began to consult together; when on a sudden a wave threw on the shore a beautiful white
stone that looked like an egg. Then the bear

said, " That's a lucky thing: this is the wonderful stone, and whoever has it may have
every thing else that he wishes." So the man
went and picked up the stone, and wished for
a palace and a garden, and a stud of horses;
and his wish was fulfilled as soon as he had
made it. And there he lived in his castle and
garden, with fine stables and horses; and all
was so grand and beautiful, that he never could
wonder and gaze at it enough.

After some time, some merchants passed
by that way. " See," said they, " what a
princely palace! The last time we were here,
it was nothing but a desert waste." They
were very curious to know how all this had
happened, and went in and asked the master of
the palace how it had been so quickly raised.
" I have done nothing myself," answered he,
" it is the wonderful stone that did all."—
" What a strange stone that must be !" said
they: then he invited them in and showed it
to them. They asked him whether he would
sell it, and offered him all their goods for it;
and the goods seemed so fine and costly, that
he quite forgot that the stone would bring him

in a moment a thousand better and richer things, and he agreed to make the bargain.

Scarcely was the stone, however, out of his hands before all his riches were gone, and he found himself sitting in his box in the water, with his jug of water and loaf of bread by his side. The grateful beasts, the mouse, the ass, and the bear, came directly to help him; but the mouse found she could not nibble off the lock this time, for it was a great deal stronger than before. Then the bear said, " We must find the wonderful stone again, or all we can do will be fruitless."

The merchants, meantime, had taken up their abode in the palace; so away went the three friends, and when they came near, the bear said, " Mouse, go in and look through the key-hole and see where the stone is kept: you are small, nobody will see you." The mouse did as she was told, but soon came back and said, " Bad news! I have looked in, and the stone hangs under the looking-glass by a red silk string, and on each side of it sits a great cat with fiery eyes to watch it."

Then the others took council together, and

said, " Go back again, and wait till the master of the palace is in bed asleep, then nip his nose and pull his hair." Away went the mouse, and did as they directed her; and the master jumped up very angry, and rubbed his nose, and cried, " Those rascally cats are good for nothing at all, they let the mice eat my very nose and pull the hair off my head." Then he hunted them out of the room; and so the mouse had the best of the game.

Next night as soon as the master was asleep, the mouse crept in again, and nibbled at the red silken string to which the stone hung, till down it dropped, and she rolled it along to the door; but when it got there, the poor little mouse was quite tired, and said to the ass, " Put in your foot, and lift it over the threshold." This was soon done : and they took up the stone, and set off for the water side. Then the ass said, " How shall we reach the box ?" " That is easily managed," answered the bear: "I can swim very well, and do you, donkey, put your fore feet over my shoulders ;— mind and hold fast, and take the stone in your mouth: as for you, mouse, you can sit in my ear."

E

It was all settled thus, and away they swam. After a time, the bear began to brag and boast: "We are brave fellows, are not we, ass?" said he; "what do you think?" But the ass held his tongue, and said not a word. "Why don't you answer me?" said the bear, "you must be an ill-mannered brute not to speak when you're spoken to." When the ass heard this, he could hold no longer; so he opened his mouth, and dropped the wonderful stone. "I could not speak," said he; "did not you know I had the stone in my mouth? now 'tis lost, and that's your fault." "Do but hold your tongue and be quiet," said the bear; "and let us think what's to be done."

Then a council was held: and at last they called together all the frogs, their wives and families, relations and friends, and said: "A great enemy is coming to eat you all up; but never mind, bring us up plenty of stones, and we'll build a strong wall to guard you." The frogs hearing this were dreadfully frightened, and set to work, bringing up all the stones they could find. At last came a large fat frog pulling along the wonderful stone by the silken string: and when the bear saw it, he jumped for joy, and said, "Now we have found what we wanted." So he released the old frog from his load, and told him to tell his friends they might go about their business as soon as they pleased.

Then the three friends swam off again for the box; and the lid flew open, and they found that they were but just in time, for the bread was all eaten, and the jug almost empty. But as soon as the good man had the stone in his hand, he wished himself safe and sound in his palace again; and in a moment there he was, with his garden and his stables and his horses; and his three faithful friends dwelt with him, and they all spent their time happily and merrily as long as they lived.

JORINDA AND JORINDEL.

There was once an old castle that stood in the middle of a large thick wood, and in the castle lived an old fairy. All the day long she flew about in the form of an owl, or crept about the country like a cat; but at night she always became an old woman again. When any youth came within a hundred paces of her castle, he became quite fixed, and could not move a step till she came and set him free: but when any pretty maiden came within that distance, she was changed into a bird; and the fairy put her into a cage and hung her up in a chamber in the castle. There were seven hundred of these cages hanging in the castle, and all with beautiful birds in them.

Now there was once a maiden whose name was Jorinda: she was prettier than all the pretty girls that ever were seen; and a shepherd whose name was Jorindel was very fond of her, and they were soon to be married. One day they went to walk in the wood, that they might be alone: and Jorindel said, " We must take care that we don't go too near to the castle." It was a beautiful evening; the last rays of the setting sun shone bright through the long stems of the trees upon the green underwood beneath, and the turtledoves sang plaintively from the tall birches.

Jorinda sat down to gaze upon the sun;

Jorindel sat by her side; and both felt sad, they knew not why; but it seemed as if they were to be parted from one another for ever. They had wandered a long way; and when they looked to see which way they should go home, they found themselves at a loss to know what path to take.

The sun was setting fast, and already half of his circle had disappeared behind the hill: Jorindel on a sudden looked behind him, and as he saw through the bushes that they had, without knowing it, sat down close under the old walls of the castle, he shrank for fear, turned pale, and trembled.   Jorinda was singing,

> The ring-dove sang from the willow spray,
>   Well-a-day ! well-a-day !
> He mourn'd for the fate
> Of his lovely mate,
>   Well-a-day ! —

The song ceased suddenly.   Jorindel turned to see the reason, and beheld his Jorinda changed into a nightingale; so that her song ended with a mournful *jug, jug*. An owl with fiery eyes flew three times round them, and three times screamed Tu whu ! Tu whu ! Tu whu! Jorindel could not move: he stood fixed as a stone, and could neither weep, nor speak, nor stir hand or foot. And now the sun went quite down; the gloomy night came; the owl flew into a bush; and a moment after the old fairy came forth pale and meager, with staring eyes, and a nose and chin that almost met one another.

She mumbled something to herself, seized the nightingale, and went away with it in her hand. Poor Jorindel saw the nightingale was gone,—but what could he do? he could not speak, he could not move from the spot where he stood. At last the fairy came back, and sung with a hoarse voice,

> Till the prisoner's fast,
> And her doom is cast,
>   There stay! Oh, stay!
> When the charm is around her,
> And the spell has bound her,
>   Hie away! away!

On a sudden Jorindel found himself free. Then he fell on his knees before the fairy, and prayed her to give him back his dear Jorinda:

but she said he should never see her again, and went her way.

He prayed, he wept, he sorrowed, but all in vain. " Alas ! " he said, " what will become of me?"

He could not return to his own home, so he went to a strange village, and employed himself in keeping sheep. Many a time did he walk round and round as near to the hated castle as he dared go. At last he dreamt one night that he found a beautiful purple flower, and in the middle of it lay a costly pearl; and he dreamt that he plucked the flower, and went with it in his hand into the castle, and that every thing he touched with it was disenchanted, and that there he found his dear Jorinda again.

In the morning when he awoke, he began to search over hill and dale for this pretty flower; and eight long days he sought for it in vain: but on the ninth day early in the morning he found the beautiful purple flower; and in the middle of it was a large dew drop as big as a costly pearl.

Then he plucked the flower, and set out and

travelled day and night till he came sgain to
the castle. He walked nearer than a hundred
paces to it, and yet he did not become fixφd
as before, but found that he could go close up
to the door.

Jorindel was very glad to see this: he touched the door with the flower, and it sprang
open, so that he went in through the court,
and listened when he heard so many birds
singing. At last he came to the chamber where
the fairy sat, with the seven hundred birds
singing in the seven hundred cages. And when
she saw Jorindel she was very angry, and
screamed with rage; but she could not come
within two yards of him; for the flower he
held in his hand protected him. He looked
around at the birds, but alas! there were
many many nightingales, and how then should
he find his Jorinda? While he was thinking
what to do, he observed that the fairy had
taken down one of the cages, and was making
her escape through the door. He ran or flew
to her, touched the cage with the flower,—
and his Jorinda stood before him. She threw
her arms round his neck and looked as beau-

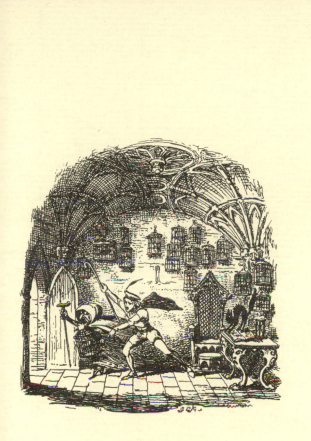

tiful as ever, as beautiful as when they walked together in the wood.

Then he touched all the other birds with the flower, so that they resumed their old forms; and took his dear Jorinda home, where they lived happily together many years.

THE WAGGISH MUSICIAN.

ONE day a waggish musician, who played delightfully on the fiddle, went rambling in a forest in a merry mood. Then he said to himself, " Time goes rather heavily on, I must find a companion." So he took up his fiddle, and fiddled away till the wood resounded with his music.

Presently up came a wolf. "Dear me! there's a wolf coming to see me," said the musician. But the wolf came up to him, and said, " How very prettily you play! I wish you would teach me." "That is easily done," said the musician, " if you will only do what I bid you." "Yes,"

replied the wolf, " I shall be a very apt scholar." So they went on a little way together,
and came at last to an old oak tree that was
hollow within, and had a large crack in the
middle of the trunk. " Look there," said the
musician, " if you wish to learn to fiddle, put
your fore feet into that crack." The wolf did
as he was bid: but the musician picked up a
large stone and wedged both his fore-feet fast
into the crack, so as to make him a prisoner.
" Now be so good as to wait there till I come
back," said he, and jogged on.

After a while, he said again to himself,
" Time goes very heavily, I must find another
companion." So he took his fiddle, and fiddled
away again in the wood. Presently up came
a fox that was wandering close by. " Ah!
there is a fox," said he. The fox came up and
said, " You delightful musician, how prettily
you play! I must and will learn to play as
you do." " That you may soon do," said the
musician, " if you do as I tell you." " That
I will," said the fox. So they travelled on
together till they came to a narrow footpath
with high bushes on each side. Then the

musician bent a stout hazel stem down to the
ground from one side of the path, and set his
foot on the top, and held it fast; and bent another from the other side, and said to the fox,
" Now, pretty fox, if you want to fiddle, give
me hold of your left paw." So the fox gave
him his paw; and he tied it fast to the top of
one of the hazel stems. " Now give me your
right," said he; and the fox did as he was
told: then the musician tied that paw to the
other hazel; and took off his foot, and away
up flew the bushes, and the fox too, and hung
sprawling and swinging in the air. " Now
be so kind as to stay there till I come back,"
said the musician, and jogged on.

But he soon said to himself, " Time begins
to hang heavy, I must find a companion." So
he took up his fiddle, and fiddled away di-
vinely. Then up came a hare running along.
" Ah ! there is a hare," said the musician.
And the hare said to him, " You fine fiddler,
how beautifully you play! will you teach me?"
" Yes," said the musician," " I will soon do
that, if you will follow my orders." " Yes,"
said the hare, " I shall make a good scholar."

Then they went on together very well for a long while, till they came to an open space in the wood. The musician tied a string round the hare's neck, and fastened the other end to the tree. " Now," said he, " pretty hare, quick, jump about, run round the tree twenty times." So the silly hare did as she was bid: and when she had run twenty times round the tree, she had twisted the string twenty times round the trunk, and was fast prisoner; and she might pull and pull away as long as she pleased, and only pulled the string faster about her neck. " Now wait there till I come back," said the musician.

But the wolf had pulled and bitten and scratched at the stone a long while, till at last he had got his feet out and was at liberty. Then he said in a great passion, " I will run after that rascally musician and tear him in pieces." As the fox saw him run by, he said, " Ah, brother wolf, pray let me down, the musician has played tricks with me." So the wolf set to work at the bottom of the hazel stem, and bit it in two; and away went both together to find the musician: and as they

came to the hare, she cried out too for help.
So they went and set her free, and all followed
the enemy together.

Meantime the musician had been fiddling
away, and found another companion; for a
poor woodcutter had been pleased with the
music, and could not help following him with
his axe under his arm. The musician was
pleased to get a man for his companion, and
behaved very civilly to him, and played him
no tricks, but stopped and played his prettiest
tunes till his heart overflowed for joy. While
the woodcutter was standing listening, he saw
the wolf, the fox, and the hare coming, and
knew by their faces that they were in a great
rage, and coming to do some mischief. So he
stood before the musician with his great axe,
as much as to say, No one shall hurt him as
long as I have this axe. And when the beasts
saw this, they were so frightened that they
ran back into the wood. Then the musician
played the woodcutter one of his best tunes
for his pains, and went on with his journey.

THE QUEEN BEE.

Two king's sons once upon a time went out into the world to seek their fortunes; but they soon fell into a wasteful foolish way of living, so that they could not return home again. Then their young brother, who was a little insignificant dwarf, went out to seek for his brothers: but when he had found them they only laughed at him, to think that he, who was so young and simple, should try to travel through the world, when they, who were so much wiser, had been unable to get on. However, they all set out on their journey together, and came at last to an ant-hill. The two elder brothers would have pulled it down, in order to see how the poor ants in their fright would run about and carry off their eggs. But the little dwarf said, "Let the poor things enjoy themselves, I will not suffer you to trouble them."

So on they went, and came to a lake where many many ducks were swimming about. The two brothers wanted to catch two, and roast them. But the dwarf said, " Let the poor things enjoy themselves, you shall not kill them." Next they came to a bees' nest in a hollow tree, and there was so much honey that it ran down the trunk; and the two brothers wanted to light a fire under the tree and kill the bees, so as to get their honey. But the dwarf held them back, and said, " Let the pretty insects enjoy themselves, I cannot let you burn them."

At length the three brothers came to a castle: and as they passed by the stables they saw fine horses standing there, but all were of marble, and no man was to be seen. Then they went through all the rooms, till they came to a door on which were three locks: but in the middle of the door there was a wicket, so that they could look into the next room. There they saw a little grey old man sitting at a table; and they called to him once or twice, but he did not hear: however, they called a third time, and then he rose and came out to them.

He said nothing, but took hold of them and led them to a beautiful table covered with all sorts of good things: and when they had eaten and drunk, he showed each of them to a bed-chamber.

The next morning he came to the eldest and took him to a marble table, where were three tablets, containing an account of the means by which the castle might be disenchanted. The first tablet said—" In the wood, under the moss, lie the thousand pearls belonging to the king's daughter; they must all be found: and if one be missing by set of sun, he who seeks them will be turned into marble."

The eldest brother set out, and sought for the pearls the whole day; but the evening came, and he had not found the first hundred: so he was turned into stone as the tablet had foretold.

The next day the second brother undertook the task; but he succeeded no better than the first; for he could only find the second hundred of the pearls; and therefore he too was turned into stone.

At last came the little dwarf's turn: and he looked in the moss; but it was so hard to find the pearls, and the job was so tiresome!—so he sat down upon a stone and cried. And as he sat there, the king of the ants (whose life he had saved) came to help him, with five thousand ants; and it was not long before they had found all the pearls and laid them in a heap.

The second tablet said—" The key of the princess's bedchamber must be fished up out of the lake." And as the dwarf came to the brink of it, he saw the two ducks whose lives he had saved swimming about; and they dived down and soon brought up the key from the bottom.

The third task was the hardest. It was to choose out the youngest and the best of the king's three daughters. Now they were all beautiful, and all exactly alike: but he was told that the eldest had eaten a piece of sugar, the next some sweet syrup, and the youngest a spoonful of honey; so he was to guess which it was that had eaten the honey.

Then came the queen of the bees, who had been saved by the little dwarf from the fire, and she tried the lips of all three; but at last she sat upon the lips of the one that had eaten the honey: and so the dwarf knew which was the youngest. Thus the spell was broken, and all who had been turned into stones awoke, and took their proper forms.   And the dwarf married the youngest and the best of the princesses, and was king after her father's death; but his two brothers married the other two sisters.

THE DOG AND THE SPARROW.

A SHEPHERD'S dog had a master who took no care of him, but often let him suffer the greatest hunger.   At last he could bear it no longer; so he took to his heels, and off he ran in a very sad and sorrowful mood.   On the road he met a sparrow, that said to him, " Why are you so sad, my friend?"   " Because," said the dog, " I am very very hungry, and have nothing to eat."   " If that be all," answered the sparrow, " come with me into the next town, and I will soon find you plenty of food."   So on they went together into the town: and as they passed by a butcher's shop, the sparrow said to the dog, " Stand there a little while, till I peck you down a piece of meat." So the sparrow perched upon the shelf: and having first looked carefully about her to see if any one was watching her, she pecked and scratched at a steak that lay upon the edge of the shelf, till at last down it fell. Then the dog snapped it up, and scrambled away with it into a corner, where he soon ate it all up. " Well," said the sparrow, " you shall have some more if you will; so come with me to the next shop, and I will peck you down another steak." When the dog had eaten this too, the sparrow said to him, " Well, my good friend, have you had enough now?" " I have had plenty of meat," answered he, " but I should like to. have a piece of bread to eat after it." " Come with me then," said the sparrow, " and you shall soon have that too." So she took him to a baker's shop, and pecked at two rolls that lay in the window, till they fell down: and as the dog still wished for more, she took him to another shop and pecked down some more for him. When that was eaten, the sparrow asked him whether he had had enough now. " Yes," said he; " and now let us take a walk a little way out of the town." So they both went out upon the high road: but as the weather was warm, they had not gone far before the dog said, " I am very much tired,—I should like to take a nap." " Very well," answered the sparrow, " do so, and in the mean time I will perch upon that bush." So the dog stretched himself out on the road, and fell fast asleep. Whilst he slept, there came by a carter with a cart drawn by three horses, and loaded with two casks of wine. The sparrow, seeing that the carter did not turn out of the way, but would go on in the track in which the dog lay, so as to drive over him, called out, " Stop! stop! Mr. Carter, or it shall be the worse for you." But the carter, grumbling to himself " You make it the worse for me, indeed! what can you do?" cracked his whip, and drove his cart over the poor dog, so that the wheels crushed him to death. " There," cried the sparrow, " thou cruel villain, thou hast killed my friend the dog. Now mind what I say. This deed of thine shall cost thee all thou art worth." " Do your worst, and welcome," said the brute, " what harm can you do me?" and passed on.

But the sparrow crept under the tilt of the cart, and pecked at the bung of one of the casks till she loosened it; and then all the wine ran out, without the carter seeing it. At last he looked round, and saw that the cart was dripping, and the cask quite empty. " What an unlucky wretch I am!" cried he. " Not wretch enough yet!" said the sparrow, as she alighted upon the head of one of the horses, and pecked at him till he reared up and kicked. When the carter saw this, he drew out his hatchet and aimed a blow at the sparrow, meaning to kill her; but she flew away, and the blow fell upon the poor horse's head with such force, that he fell down dead. " Unlucky wretch that I am!" cried he. " Not wretch enough yet!" said the sparrow. And as the carter went on with the other two horses, she again crept under the tilt of the cart, and pecked out the bung of the second cask, so that all the wine ran out. When the carter saw this, he again cried out, " Miserable wretch that I am!" But the sparrow answered, " Not wretch enough yet!" and perched on the head of the second horse, and pecked at him too. The carter ran up and struck at her again with his hatchet; but away she flew, and the blow fell upon the second horse and killed him on the spot. "Unlucky wretch that I am!" said he. "Not wretch enough yet!" said the sparrow; and perching upon the third horse, she began to peck him too. The carrier was mad with fury; and without looking about him, or caring what he was about, struck again at the sparrow; but killed his third horse as he had done the other two. "Alas! miserable wretch that I am!" cried he. "Not wretch enough yet!" answered the sparrow as she flew away; "now will I plague and punish thee at thy own house." The carter was forced at last to leave his cart behind him, and to go home overflowing with rage and vexation. "Alas!" said he to his wife, "what ill luck has befallen me!—my wine is all spilt, and my horses all three dead." "Alas! husband," replied she, "and a wicked bird has come into the house, and has brought with her all the birds in the world, I am sure, and they have fallen upon our corn in the loft, and are eating it up at such a rate!" Away ran the husband up stairs, and saw thousands of birds sitting upon the floor eating up his corn, with the sparrow in the midst of them. " Un- lucky wretch that I am ! " cried the carter; for he saw that the corn was almost all gone. " Not wretch enough yet! " said the sparrow; " thy cruelty shall cost thee thy life yet! " and away she flew.

The carter seeing that he had thus lost all that he had, went down into his kitchen; and was still not sorry for what he had done, but sat himself angrily and sulkily in the chimney corner. But the sparrow sat on the outside of the window, and cried, " Carter ! thy cruelty shall cost thee thy life! " With that he jumped up in a rage, seized his hatchet, and threw it at the sparrow ; but it missed her, and only broke the window. The sparrow now hopped in, perched upon the window-seat, and cried, " Carter! it shall cost thee thy life! " Then he became mad and blind with rage, and struck the window seat with such force that he cleft it in two: and as the sparrow flew from place to place, the carter and his wife were so fu- rious, that they broke all their furniture, glasses, chairs, benches, the table, and at last the walls,

without touching the bird at all. In the end,
however, they caught her: and the wife said,
" Shall I kill her at once?" " No," cried he,
" that is letting her off too easily: she shall
die a much more cruel death ; I will eat her."
But the sparrow began to flutter about, and
stretched out her neck and cried, " Carter! it
shall cost thee thy life yet!" With that he
could wait no longer: so he gave his wife the
hatchet, and cried, " Wife, strike at the bird
and kill her in my hand." And the wife struck;
but she missed her aim, and hit her husband
on the head so that he fell down dead, and the
sparrow flew quietly home to her nest.

FREDERICK AND CATHERINE.

THERE was once a man called Frederick:
he had a wife whose name was Catherine, and
they had not long been married. One day
Frederick said, " Kate! I am going to work
in the fields; when I come back I shall be

hungry, so let me have something nice cooked,
and a good draught of ale." " Very well," said
she, " it shall all be ready."   When dinner-
time drew nigh, Catherine took a nice steak,
which was all the meat she had, and put it on
the fire to fry. The steak soon began to look
brown, and to crackle in the pan; and Catherine stood by with a fork and turned it: then
she said to herself, " The steak is almost ready,
I may as well go to the cellar for the ale."   So
she left the pan on the fire, and took a large jug
and went into the cellar and tapped the ale
cask. The beer ran into the jug, and Catherine
stood looking on.   At last it popped into her
head, " The dog is not shut up—he may be
running away with the steak; that's well
thought of."   So up she ran from the cellar;
and sure enough the rascally cur had got the
steak in his mouth, and was making off with
it.

Away ran Catherine, and away ran the dog
across the field: but he ran faster than she,
and stuck close to the steak.   " It's all gone,
and ' what can't be cured must be endured,' "
said Catherine. So she turned round; and as

she had run a good way and was tired, she
walked home leisurely to cool herself.

Now all this time the ale was running too,
for Catherine had not turned the cock; and
when the jug was full the liquor ran upon the
floor till the cask was empty. When she got
to the cellar stairs she saw what had happened.
" My stars ! " said she, " what shall I do to
keep Frederick from seeing all this slopping
about?" So she thought a while; and at last
remembered that there was a sack of fine
meal bought at the last fair, and that if she
sprinkled this over the floor it would suck
up the ale nicely. " What a lucky thing,"
said she, " that we kept that meal ! we have
now a good use for it." So away she went
for it: but she managed to set it down just
upon the great jug full of beer, and upset it;
and thus all the ale that had been saved was
set swimming on the floor also. " Ah ! well,"
said she, " when one goes, another may as
well follow." Then she strewed the meal all
about the cellar, and was quite pleased with
her cleverness, and said, " How very neat and
clean it looks ! "

At noon Frederick came home. " Now, wife," cried he, " what have you for dinner?" " O Frederick!" answered she, " I was cooking you a steak; but while I went down to draw the ale, the dog ran away with it; and while I ran after him, the ale all ran out; and when I went to dry up the ale with the sack of meal that we got at the fair, I upset the jug: but the cellar is now quite dry, and looks so clean!" " Kate, Kate," said he, " how could you do all this? Why did you leave the steak to fry, and the ale to run, and then spoil all the meal?" " Why, Frederick," said she, " I did not know that I was doing wrong, you should have told me before."

The husband thought to himself, If my wife manages matters thus, I must look sharp myself. Now he had a good deal of gold in the house: so he said to Catherine, " What pretty yellow buttons these are! I shall put them into a box and bury them in the garden; but take care that you never go near or meddle with them." " No, Frederick," said she, " that I never will." As soon as he was gone, there came by some pedlars with earthenware plates and dishes, and they asked her whether she would buy. " Oh dear me, I should like to buy very much, but I have no money: if you had any use for yellow buttons, I might deal with you." " Yellow buttons!" said they: " let us have a look at them." " Go into the garden and dig where I tell you, and you will find the yellow buttons: I dare not go myself." So the rogues went: and when they found what these yellow buttons were, they took them all away, and left her plenty of plates and dishes. Then she set them all about the house for a show: and when Frederick came back, he cried out, " Kate, what have you been doing?" " See," said she, " I have bought all these with your yellow buttons: but I did not touch them myself; the pedlars went themselves and dug them up." " Wife, wife," said Frederick, " what a pretty piece of work you have made! those yellow buttons were all my money: How came you to do such a thing?" " Why," answered she, " I did not know there was any harm in it; you should have told me."

Catherine stood musing for a while, and at

last said to her husband, "Hark ye, Frederick, we will soon get the gold back: let us run after the thieves." " Well, we will try," answered he; " but take some butter and cheese with you, that we may have something to eat by the way." " Very well," said she; and they set out: and as Frederick walked the fastest, he left his wife some way behind. " It does not matter," thought she: " when we turn back, I shall be so much nearer home than he."

Presently she came to the top of a hill; down the side of which there was a road so narrow that the cart-wheels always chafed the trees on each side as they passed. " Ah, see now," said she, " how they have bruised and wounded those poor trees; they will never get well." So she took pity on them, and made use of the butter to grease them all, so that the wheels might not hurt them so much. While she was doing this kind office, one of her cheeses fell out of the basket, and rolled down the hill. Catherine looked, but could not see where it was gone; so she said " Well, I suppose the other will go the same way and find you; he

has younger legs than I have." Then she
rolled the other cheese after it; and away it
went, nobody knows where, down the hill.
But she said she supposed they knew the road,
and would follow her, and she could not stay
there all day waiting for them.

At last she overtook Frederick, who desired
her to give him something to eat. Then she
gave him the dry bread. "Where are the
butter and cheese?" said he. "Oh!" answered she, "I used the butter to grease those
poor trees that the wheels chafed so: and one
of the cheeses ran away, so I sent the other
after it to find it, and I suppose they are both
on the road together somewhere." "What a
goose you are to do such silly things!" said
the husband. "How can you say so?" said
she; "I am sure you never told me not."

They ate the dry bread together; and Frederick said, "Kate, I hope you locked the
door safe when you came away?" "No," answered she, "you did not tell me." "Then go
home, and do it now before we go any further,"
said Frederick, "and bring with you something to eat."

Catherine did as he told her, and thought to herself by the way, " Frederick wants something to eat; but I don't think he is very fond of butter and cheese: I'll bring him a bag of fine nuts, and the vinegar, for I have often seen him take some."

When she reached home, she bolted the back door, but the front door she took off the hinges, and said, " Frederick told me to lock the door, but surely it can no where be so safe as if I take it with me." So she took her time by the way: and when she overtook her husband she cried out, " There, Frederick, there is the door itself, now you may watch it as carefully as you please." " Alas! alas!" said he, " what a clever wife I have ! I sent you to make the house fast, and you take the door away, so that every body may go in and out as they please:—however, as you have brought the door, you shall carry it about with you for your pains." " Very well," answered she, " I'll carry the door; but I'll not carry the nuts and vinegar bottle also,—that would be too much of a load; so, if you please, I'll fasten them to the door."

Frederick of course made no objection to that plan, and they set off into the wood to look for the thieves; but they could not find them: and when it grew dark, they climbed up into a tree to spend the night there. Scarcely were they up, than who should come by but the very rogues they were looking for. They were in truth great rascals, and belonged to that class of people who find things before they are lost: they were tired; so they sat down and made a fire under the very tree where Frederick and Catherine were. Frederick slipped down on the other side, and picked up some stones. Then he climbed up again, and tried to hit the thieves on the head with them: but they only said, " It must be near morning, for the wind shakes the fir-apples down."

Catherine, who had the door on her shoulder, began to be very tired; but she thought it was the nuts upon it that were so heavy: so she said softly, " Frederick, I must let the nuts go." " No," answered he, " not now, they will discover us." "I can't help that, they must go." " Well then, make haste and throw them down, if you will." Then away rattled the nuts down among the boughs; and one of the thieves cried, " Bless me, it is hailing."

A little while after, Catherine thought the door was still very heavy: so she whispered to Frederick, " I must throw the vinegar down." " Pray don't," answered he, " it will discover us." " I can't help that," said she, " go it must." So she poured all the vinegar down; and the thieves said, " What a heavy dew there is ! "

At last it popped into Catherine's head that it was the door itself that was so heavy all the time: so she whispered Frederick, " I must throw the door down soon." But he begged and prayed her not to do so, for he was sure it would betray them. "Here goes, however," said she: and down went the door with such a clatter upon the thieves, that they cried out " Murder!" and not knowing what was coming, ran away as fast as they could, and left all the gold. So Catherine was right at last; and when she and Frederick came down, there they found all their money safe and sound.

THREE CHILDREN OF FORTUNE.

Once upon a time a father sent for his three sons, and gave to the eldest a cock, to the second a scythe, and to the third a cat. " I am now old," said he, " my end is approaching, and I would fain provide for you before I die. Money I have none, and what I now give you seems of but little worth; yet it rests with yourselves alone to turn my gifts to good account. Only seek out for a land where what you have is as yet unknown, and your fortune is made."

After the death of the father, the eldest set out with his cock: but wherever he went, in every town he saw from afar off a cock sitting upon the church-steeple, and turning round with the wind. In the villages he always heard plenty of them crowing, and his bird was therefore nothing new; so there did not seem much chance of his making his fortune. At length it happened that he came to an island where the people who lived there had never heard of a cock, and knew not even how to reckon the time. They knew, indeed, if it were morning or evening; but at night, if they lay awake, they had no means of knowing how time went. "Behold," said he to them, "what a noble animal this is! how like a knight he is! he carries a bright red crest upon his head, and spurs upon his heels; he crows three times every night, at stated hours, and at the third time the sun is about to rise. But this is not all; sometimes he screams in broad day-light, and then you must take warning, for the weather is surely about to change." This pleased the natives mightily; they kept awake one whole night, and heard, to their great joy, how gloriously the cock called the hour, at two, four, and six o'clock. Then they asked him whether the bird was to be sold, and how much he would sell it for. "About as much gold as an ass can carry," said he. "A very fair price for such an animal," cried they with one voice; and agreed to give him what he asked.

When he returned home with his wealth, his brothers wondered greatly: and the second

said, " I will now set forth likewise, and see if
I can turn my scythe to as good an account."
There did not seem, however, much likelihood
of this; for go where he would, he was met by
peasants who had as good a scythe on their
shoulders as he had. But at last, as good luck
would have it, he came to an island where the
people had never heard of a scythe: there, as
soon as the corn was ripe, they went into the
fields and pulled it up; but this was very hard
work, and a great deal of it was lost. The
man then set to work with his scythe; and
mowed down their whole crop so quickly, that
the people stood staring open-mouthed with
wonder. They were willing to give him what
he asked for such a marvellous thing: but he
only took a horse laden with as much gold as
it could carry.

Now the third brother had a great longing
to go and see what he could make of his cat.
So he set out: and at first it happened to him
as it had to the others, so long as he kept upon
the main land, he met with no success; there
were plenty of cats every where, indeed too
many, so that the young ones were for the most

part, as soon as they came into the world, drowned in the water. At last he passed over to an island, where, as it chanced most luckily for him, nobody had ever seen a cat; and they were overrun with mice to such a degree, that the little wretches danced upon the tables and chairs, whether the master of the house were at home or not. The people complained loudly of this grievance; the king himself knew not how to rid himself of them in his palace; in every corner mice were squeaking, and they gnawed every thing that their teeth could lay hold of. Here was a fine field for Puss—she soon began her chase, and had cleared two rooms in the twinkling of an eye; when the people besought their king to buy the wonderful animal, for the good of the public, at any price. The king willingly gave what was asked,—a mule laden with gold and jewels; and thus the third brother returned home with a richer prize than either of the others.

Meantime the cat feasted away upon the mice in the royal palace, and devoured so many that they were no longer in any great numbers. At length, quite spent and tired with her work, she became extremely thirsty; so she stood still, drew up her head, and cried " Miau, Miau!" The king gathered together all his subjects when they heard this strange cry, and many ran shrieking in a great fright out of the palace. But the king held a council below as to what was best to be done; and it was at length fixed to send a herald to the cat, to warn her to leave the castle forthwith, or that force would be used to remove her. "For," said the counsellors, "we would far more willingly put up with the mice (since we are used to that evil), than get rid of them at the risk of our lives." A page accordingly went, and asked the cat " whether she were willing to quit the castle?" But Puss, whose thirst became every moment more and more pressing, answered nothing but " Miau! Miau!" which the page interpreted to mean " No! No!" and therefore carried this answer to the king. " Well," said the counsellors, " then we must try what force will do." So the guns were planted, and the palace was fired upon from all sides. When the fire reached the room where the cat was, she sprang out of the win-

dow and ran away; but the besiegers did not
see her, and went on firing until the whole
palace was burnt to the ground.

KING GRISLY-BEARD.

A GREAT king had a daughter who was very
beautiful, but so proud and haughty and con-
ceited, that none of the princes who came to
ask her in marriage were good enough for her,
and she only made sport of them.

Once upon a time the king held a great
feast, and invited all her suitors; and they sat
in a row according to their rank, kings and
princes and dukes and earls. Then the princess came in and passed by them all, but she
had something spiteful to say to every one.
The first was too fat: "He's as round as a tub,"
said she. The next was too tall: " What a
maypole!" said she. The next was too short:
" What a dumpling!" said she. The fourth
was too pale, and she called him "Wallface."

The fifth was too red, so she called him
" Cockscomb." The sixth was not straight
enough, so she said he was like a green stick
that had been laid to dry over a baker's oven.
And thus she had some joke to crack upon
every one: but she laughed more than all at
a good king who was there. " Look at him,"
said she, " his beard is like an old mop, he
shall be called Grisly-beard." So the king
got the nick-name of Grisly-beard.

But the old king was very angry when he
saw how his daughter behaved, and how she
ill-treated all his guests; and he vowed that,
willing or unwilling, she should marry the first
beggar that came to the door.

Two days after there came by a travelling
musician, who began to sing under the window, and beg alms: and when the king heard
him, he said, " Let him come in." So they
brought in a dirty-looking fellow; and when
he had sung before the king and the princess,
he begged a boon. Then the king said, " You
have sung so well, that I will give you my
daughter for your wife." The princess begged and prayed; but the king said, " I have

sworn to give you to the first beggar, and I will keep my word." So words and tears were of no avail; the parson was sent for, and she was married to the musician. When this was over, the king said, " Now get ready to go ; you must not stay here; you must travel on with your husband."

Then the beggar departed, and took her with him ; and they soon came to a great wood. " Pray," said she, " whose is this wood?" " It belongs to king Grisly-beard," answered he; "hadst thou taken him, all had been thine." " Ah ! unlucky wretch that I am ! " sighed she, " would that I had married king Grisly-beard !" Next they came to some fine meadows. " Whose are these beautiful green meadows?" said she. " They belong to king Grisly-beard ; hadst thou taken him, they had all been thine." " Ah ! unlucky wretch that I am !" said she, "would that I had married king Grisly-beard !"

Then they came to a great city. " Whose is this noble city?" said she. " It belongs to king Grisly-beard; hadst thou taken him, it had all been thine." " Ah ! miserable wretch

that I am!" sighed she, "why did I not marry
king Grisly-beard?" "That is no business of
mine," said the musician; "why should you
wish for another husband? am not I good
enough for you?"

At last they came to a small cottage. "What
a paltry place!" said she; "to whom does that
little dirty hole belong?" The musician answered, "That is your and my house, where
we are to live." "Where are your servants?"
cried she. "What do we want with servants?"
said he, "you must do for yourself whatever
is to be done. Now make the fire, and put on
water and cook my supper, for I am very tired."
But the princess knew nothing of making fires
and cooking, and the beggar was forced to help
her. When they had eaten a very scanty meal
they went to bed; but the musician called her
up very early in the morning to clean the house.
Thus they lived for two days: and when they
had eaten up all there was in the cottage, the
man said, "Wife, we can't go on thus, spending
money and earning nothing. You must learn
to weave baskets." Then he went out and cut
willows and brought them home, and she began

to weave; but it made her fingers very sore. "I see this work won't do," said he, "try and spin; perhaps you will do that better." So she sat down and tried to spin; but the threads cut her tender fingers till the blood ran. "See now," said the musician, "you are good for nothing, you can do no work;—what a bargain I have got! However, I'll try and set up a trade in pots and pans, and you shall stand in the market and sell them." "Alas!" sighed she, "when I stand in the market and any of my father's court pass by and see me there, how they will laugh at me!"

But the beggar did not care for that; and said she must work, if she did not wish to die of hunger. At first the trade went well; for many people, seeing such a beautiful woman, went to buy her wares, and paid their money without thinking of taking away the goods. They lived on this as long as it lasted, and then her husband bought a fresh lot of ware, and she sat herself down with it in the corner of the market; but a drunken soldier soon came by, and rode his horse against her stall and broke all her goods into a thousand pieces. Then

she began to weep, and knew not what to do.
" Ah! what will become of me!" said she;
"what will my husband say?" So she ran home
and told him all. " Who would have thought
you would have been so silly," said he, " as
to put an earthenware stall in the corner of the
market, where every body passes?—But let
us have no more crying; I see you are not fit
for this sort of work: so I have been to the
king's palace, and asked if they did not want a
kitchen-maid, and they have promised to take
you, and there you will have plenty to eat."

Thus the princess became a kitchen-maid,
and helped the cook to do all the dirtiest
work: she was allowed to carry home some of
the meat that was left, and on this she and
her husband lived.

She had not been there long, before she heard
that the king's eldest son was passing by, going
to be married; and she went to one of the
windows and looked out. Every thing was
ready, and all the pomp and splendour of the
court was there. Then she thought with an
aching heart on her own sad fate, and bitterly
grieved for the pride and folly which had

brought her so low. And the servants gave her some of the rich meats, which she put into her basket to take home.

All on a sudden, as she was going out, in came the king's son in golden clothes; and when he saw a beautiful woman at the door, he took her by the hand, and said she should be his partner in the dance: but she trembled for fear, for she saw that it was king Grisly-beard, who was making sport of her. However, he kept fast hold and led her in; and the cover of the basket came off, so that the meats in it fell all about. Then everybody laughed and jeered at her; and she was so abashed that she wished herself a thousand feet deep in the earth. She sprang to the door to run away; but on the steps king Grisly-beard overtook and brought her back, and said, " Fear me not! I am the musician who has lived with you in the hut : I brought you there because I loved you. I am also the soldier who overset your stall. I have done all this only to cure you of pride, and to punish you for the ill-treatment you bestowed on me. Now all is over; you have learnt wisdom, your faults are gone, and it is time to celebrate our marriage feast!"

Then the chamberlains came and brought her the most beautiful robes: and her father and his whole court were there already, and congratulated her on her marriage. Joy was in every face. The feast was grand, and all were merry; and I wish you and I had been of the party.

THE ADVENTURES

OF

CHANTICLEER AND PARTLET.

1. *How they went to the Mountains to eat Nuts.*

"THE nuts are quite ripe now," said Chanticleer to his wife Partlet, "suppose we go together to the mountains, and eat as many as we can, before the squirrel takes them all away." "With all my heart," said Partlet, "let us go and make a holiday of it together."

So they went to the mountains; and as it was a lovely day they stayed there till the evening. Now, whether it was that they had eaten so many nuts that they could not walk, or whether they were lazy and would not, I do not know: however, they took it into their heads that it did not become them to go home on foot. So Chanticleer began to build a little carriage of nut-shells: and when it was finished, Partlet jumped into it and sat down, and bid Chanticleer harness himself to it and draw her home. "That's a good joke!" said Chanticleer; "no, that will never do; I had rather by half walk home; I'll sit on the box and be coachman, if you like, but I'll not draw." While this was passing, a duck came quacking up, and cried out, "You thieving vagabonds, what business have you in my grounds? I'll give it you well for your insolence!" and upon that she fell upon Chanticleer most lustily. But Chanticleer was no coward, and returned the duck's blows with his sharp spurs so fiercely, that she soon began to cry out for mercy; which was only granted her upon condition that she would draw the carriage home for them. This she agreed to do; and Chanticleer got upon the box, and drove, crying, " Now, duck, get on as fast as you can." And away they went at a pretty good pace.

After they had travelled along a little way, they met a needle and a pin walking together along the road: and the needle cried out, " Stop! stop!" and said it was so dark that they could hardly find their way, and such dirty walking they could not get on at all: he told them that he and his friend, the pin, had been at a public house a few miles off, and had sat drinking till they had forgotten how late it was; he begged therefore that the travellers would be so kind as to give them a lift in their carriage. Chanticleer, observing that they were but thin fellows, and not likely to take up much room, told them they might ride, but made them promise not to dirty the wheels of the carriage in getting in, nor to tread on Partlet's toes.

Late at night they arrived at an inn; and as it was bad travelling in the dark, and the duck seemed much tired, and waddled about a good deal from one side to the other, they made up

their minds to fix their quarters there; but
the landlord at first was unwilling, and said
his house was full, thinking they might not
be very respectable company: however, they
spoke civilly to him, and gave him the egg
which Partlet had laid by the way, and said
they would give him the duck, who was in
the habit of laying one every day: so at last
he let them come in, and they bespoke a
handsome supper, and spent the evening very
jollily.

Early in the morning, before it was quite
light, and when no body was stirring in the inn,
Chanticleer awakened his wife, and, fetching
the egg, they pecked a hole in it, ate it up, and
threw the shells into the fire-place. They then
went to the pin and needle, who were fast asleep,
and, seizing them by their heads, stuck one
into the landlord's easy chair, and the other
into his handkerchief: having done this, they
crept away as softly as possible. However,
the duck, who slept in the open air in the
yard, heard them coming, and jumping into
the brook which ran close by the inn, soon
swam out of their reach.

G

An hour or two afterwards the landlord got up, and took his handkerchief to wipe his face, but the pin ran into him and pricked him: then he walked into the kitchen to light his pipe at the fire, but when he stirred it up the egg-shells flew into his eyes, and almost blinded him. "Bless me!" said he, "all the world seems to have a design against my head this morning:" and so saying, he threw himself sulkily into his easy chair; but, oh dear! the needle ran into him; and this time the pain was not in his head. He now flew into a very great passion, and, suspecting the company who had come in the night before, went to look after them, but they were all off; so he swore that he never again would take in such a troop of vagabonds, who ate a great deal, paid no reckoning, and gave him nothing for his trouble but their apish tricks.

2. *How Chanticleer and Partlet went to visit Mr. Korbés.*

Another day, Chanticleer and Partlet wished to ride out together; so Chanticleer built a handsome carriage with four red wheels, and harnessed six mice to it; and then he and Partlet got into the carriage, and away they drove. Soon afterwards a cat met them, and said, " Where are you going?" And Chanticleer replied,

> " All on our way
> A visit to pay
> To Mr. Korbes, the fox, to-day."

Then the cat said, " Take me with you." Chanticleer said, " With all my heart: get up behind, and be sure you do not fall off."

> " Take care of this handsome coach of mine,
> Nor dirty my pretty red wheels so fine !
> Now, mice, be ready,
> And, wheels, run steady !
> For we are going a visit to pay
> To Mr. Korbes, the fox, to-day."

Soon after came up a mill-stone, an egg, a duck, and a pin; and Chanticleer gave them all leave to get into the carriage and go with them.

When they arrived at Mr. Korbes's house, he was not at home; so the mice drew the carriage into the coach-house, Chanticleer and Partlet flew upon a beam, the cat sat down in the fire-place, the duck got into the washing cistern, the pin stuck himself into the bed pillow, the mill-stone laid himself over the house door, and the egg rolled herself up in the towel.

When Mr. Korbes came home, he went to the fire-place to make a fire; but the cat threw all the ashes in his eyes: so he ran to the kitchen to wash himself; but there the duck splashed all the water in his face; and when he tried to wipe himself, the egg broke to pieces in the towel all over his face and eyes. Then he was very angry, and went without his supper to bed; but when he laid his head on the pillow, the pin ran into his cheek: at this he became quite furious, and, jumping up, would have run out of the house: but when he came to the door, the mill-stone fell down on his head, and killed him on the spot.

3. *How Partlet died and was buried, and how Chanticleer died of grief.*

Another day Chanticleer and Partlet agreed to go again to the mountains to eat nuts; and it was settled that all the nuts which they found should be shared equally between them. Now Partlet found a very large nut; but she said nothing about it to Chanticleer, and kept it all to herself: however, it was so big that she could not swallow it, and it stuck in her throat. Then she was in a great fright, and cried out to Chanticleer, " Pray run as fast as you can, and fetch me some water, or I shall be choked." Chanticleer ran as fast as he could to the river, and said, " River, give me some water, for Partlet lies on the mountain, and will be choked by a great nut." The river said, " Run first to the bride, and ask her for a silken cord to draw up the water." Chanticleer ran to the bride, and said, " Bride, you must give me a silken cord, for then the river will give me water, and the water I will carry to Partlet, who lies on the mountain, and will be choked by a great nut." But the bride said, " Run first, and bring me my garland that is hanging on a willow in the garden." Then Chanticleer ran to the garden, and took the garland from the bough where it hung, and brought it to the bride; and then the bride gave him the silken cord, and he took the silken cord to the river, and the river gave him water, and he carried the water to Partlet; but in the mean time she was choked by the great nut, and lay quite dead, and never moved any more.

Then Chanticleer was very sorry, and cried bitterly; and all the beasts came and wept with him over poor Partlet. And six mice built a little hearse to carry her to her grave; and when it was ready they harnessed themselves before it, and Chanticleer drove them. On the way they met the fox. " Where are you going, Chanticleer?" said he. " To bury my Partlet," said the other. " May I go with you?" said the fox. " Yes; but you must get up behind, or my horses will not be able to draw you." Then the fox got up behind; and presently the wolf, the bear, the goat, and all the beasts of the wood, came and climbed upon the hearse.

So on they went till they came to a rapid stream. "How shall we get over?" said Chanticleer. Then said a straw, "I will lay myself across, and you may pass over upon me." But as the mice were going over, the straw slipped away and fell into the water, and the six mice all fell in and were drowned. What was to be done? Then a large log of wood came and said, "I am big enough; I will lay myself across the stream, and you shall pass over upon me." So he laid himself down; but they managed so clumsily, that the log of wood fell in and was carried away by the stream. Then a stone, who saw what had happened, came up and kindly offered to help poor Chanticleer by laying himself across the stream; and this time he got safely to the other side with the hearse, and managed to get Partlet out of it; but the fox and the other mourners, who were sitting behind, were too heavy, and fell back into the water and were all carried away by the stream, and drowned.

Thus Chanticleer was left alone with his dead Partlet; and having dug a grave for her, he laid her in it, and made a little hillock over her. Then he sat down by the grave, and wept and mourned, till at last he died too: and so all were dead.

SNOW-DROP.

It was in the middle of winter, when the broad flakes of snow were falling around, that a certain queen sat working at a window, the frame of which was made of fine black ebony; and as she was looking out upon the snow, she pricked her finger, and three drops of blood fell upon it. Then she gazed thoughtfully upon the red drops which sprinkled the white snow, and said, " Would that my little daughter may be as white as that snow, as red as the blood, and as black as the ebony window-frame!" And so the little girl grew up: her skin was as white as snow, her cheeks as rosy as the blood, and her hair as black as ebony; and she was called Snow-drop.

But this queen died; and the king soon married another wife, who was very beautiful, but so proud that she could not bear to think that any one could surpass her. She had a magical looking-glass, to which she used to go and gaze upon herself in it, and say,

> " Tell me, glass, tell me true !
> Of all the ladies in the land,
> Who is the fairest ? tell me who? "

And the glass answered,

> " Thou, queen, art fairest in the land."

But Snow-drop grew more and more beautiful; and when she was seven years old, she was as bright as the day, and fairer than the queen herself. Then the glass one day answered the queen, when she went to consult it as usual,

> " Thou, queen, may'st fair and beauteous be,
> But Snow-drop is lovelier far than thee ! "

When she heard this, she turned pale with rage and envy; and called to one of her servants and said, " Take Snow-drop away into

the wide wood, that I may never see her more."
Then the servant led her away; but his heart
melted when she begged him to spare her life,
and he said, " I will not hurt thee, thou pretty
child." So he left her by herself; and though
he thought it most likely that the wild beasts
would tear her in pieces, he felt as if a great
weight were taken off his heart when he had
made up his mind not to kill her, but leave
her to her fate.

Then poor Snow-drop wandered along
through the wood in great fear; and the wild
beasts roared about her, but none did her any
harm. In the evening she came to a little cottage, and went in there to rest herself, for her
little feet would carry her no further. Every
thing was spruce and neat in the cottage: on
the table was spread a white cloth, and there
were seven little plates with seven little loaves,
and seven little glasses with wine in them; and
knives and forks laid in order; and by the wall
stood seven little beds. Then, as she was very
hungry, she picked a little piece off each loaf,
and drank a very little wine out of each glass;
and after that she thought she would lie down

and rest. So she tried all the little beds; and one was too long, and another was too short, till at last the seventh suited her; and there she laid herself down, and went to sleep.

Presently in came the masters of the cottage, who were seven little dwarfs that lived among the mountains, and dug and searched about for gold. They lighted up their seven lamps, and saw directly that all was not right. The first said, " Who has been sitting on my stool?" The second, " Who has been eating off my plate?" The third, " Who has been picking my bread?" The fourth, " Who has been meddling with my spoon?" The fifth, " Who has been handling my fork?" The sixth, " Who was been cutting with my knife?" The seventh, " Who has been drinking my wine?" Then the first looked round and said, " Who has been lying on my bed?" And the rest came running to him, and every one cried out that somebody had been upon his bed. But the seventh saw Snow-drop, and called all his brethren to come and see her; and they cried out with wonder and astonishment, and

brought their lamps to look at her, and said,
" Good heavens ! what a lovely child she is ! "
And they were delighted to see her, and took
care not to wake her; and the seventh dwarf
slept an hour with each of the other dwarfs in
turn, till the night was gone.

In the morning, Snow-drop told them all
her story; and they pitied her, and said if she
would keep all things in order, and cook and
wash, and knit and spin for them, she might
stay where she was, and they would take good
care of her. Then they went out all day long
to their work, seeking for gold and silver in
the mountains; and Snow-drop remained at
home : and they warned her, and said, " The
queen will soon find out where you are, so
take care and let no one in."

But the queen, now that she thought Snow-
drop was dead, believed that she was certainly
the handsomest lady in the land; and she went
to her glass and said,

> " Tell me, glass, tell me true !
>   Of all the ladies in the land,
> Who is fairest ? tell me who ? "

And the glass answered,

" Thou, queen, art the fairest in all this land;
But over the hills, in the greenwood shade,
Where the seven dwarfs their dwelling have made,
There Snow-drop is hiding her head, and she
Is lovelier far, O queen! than thee."

Then the queen was very much alarmed;
for she knew that the glass always spoke the
truth, and was sure that the servant had betrayed her. And she could not bear to think
that any one lived who was more beautiful
than she was; so she disguised herself as an
old pedlar, and went her way over the hills to
the place where the dwarfs dwelt. Then she
knocked at the door, and cried " Fine wares
to sell!" Snow-drop looked out at the window, and said, " Good day, good woman;
what have you to sell?" " Good wares, fine
wares," said she; " laces and bobbins of all
colours." " I will let the old lady in; she
seems to be a very good sort of body," thought
Snow-drop; so she ran down, and unbolted
the door. " Bless me!" said the old woman,
" how badly your stays are laced! Let me
lace them up with one of my nice new laces."

Snow-drop did not dream of any mischief; so she stood up before the old woman; but she set to work so nimbly, and pulled the lace so tight, that Snow-drop lost her breath, and fell down as if she were dead. " There's an end of all thy beauty," said the spiteful queen, and went away home.

In the evening the seven dwarfs returned; and I need not say how grieved they were to see their faithful Snow-drop stretched upon the ground motionless, as if she were quite dead. However, they lifted her up, and when they found what was the matter, they cut the lace; and in a little time she began to breathe, and soon came to life again. Then they said, " The old woman was the queen herself; take care another time, and let no one in when we are away."

When the queen got home, she went straight to her glass, and spoke to it as usual; but to her great surprise it still said,

" Thou, queen, art the fairest in all this land;
But over the hills, in the greenwood shade,
Where the seven dwarfs their dwelling have made,
There Snow-drop is hiding her head; and she
Is lovelier far, O queen! than thee."

Then the blood ran cold in her heart with spite and malice to see that Snow-drop still lived; and she dressed herself up again in a disguise, but very different from the one she wore before, and took with her a poisoned comb. When she reached the dwarfs' cottage, she knocked at the door, and cried " Fine wares to sell!" But Snow-drop said, " I dare not let any one in." Then the queen said, "Only look at my beautiful combs;" and gave her the poisoned one. And it looked so pretty that she took it up and put it into her hair to try it; but the moment it touched her head the poison was so powerful that she fell down senseless. " There you may lie," said the queen, and went her way. But by good luck the dwarfs returned very early that evening; and when they saw Snow-drop lying on the ground, they thought what had happened, and soon found the poisoned comb. And when they took it away, she recovered, and told them all that had passed; and they warned her once more not to open the door to any one.

Meantime the queen went home to her glass, and trembled with rage when she received ex-

actly the same answer as before; and she said,
" Snow-drop shall die, if it costs me my life."
So she went secretly into a chamber, and prepared a poisoned apple: the outside looked
very rosy and tempting, but whoever tasted it
was sure to die. Then she dressed herself up
as a peasant's wife, and travelled over the hills
to the dwarfs' cottage, and knocked at the door;
but Snow-drop put her head out of the window and said, " I dare not let any one in, for
the dwarfs have told me not." " Do as you
please," said the old woman, " but at any rate
take this pretty apple; I will make you a present of it." " No," said Snow-drop, " I dare
not take it." " You silly girl!" answered the
other, "what are you afraid of? do you think
it is poisoned? Come! do you eat one part,
and I will eat the other." Now the apple was
so prepared that one side was good, though the
other side was poisoned. Then Snow-drop was
very much tempted to taste, for the apple looked
exceedingly nice; and when she saw the old
woman eat, she could refrain no longer. But
she had scarcely put the piece into her mouth,
when she fell down dead upon the ground.

" This time nothing will save thee," said the queen; and she went home to her glass, and at last it said

" Thou, queen, art the fairest of all the fair."

And then her envious heart was glad, and as happy as such a heart could be.

When evening came, and the dwarfs returned home, they found Snow-drop lying on the ground: no breath passed her lips, and they were afraid that she was quite dead. They lifted her up, and combed her hair, and washed her face with wine and water; but all was in vain, for the little girl seemed quite dead. So they laid her down upon a bier, and all seven watched and bewailed her three whole days; and then they proposed to bury her; but her cheeks were still rosy, and her face looked just as it did while she was alive; so they said, " We will never bury her in the cold ground." And they made a coffin of glass, so that they might still look at her, and wrote her name upon it, in golden letters, and that she was a king's daughter. And the coffin was placed upon the hill, and one of the dwarfs always sat

by it and watched. And the birds of the air
came too, and bemoaned Snow-drop: first of
all came an owl, and then a raven, but at last
came a dove.

And thus Snow-drop lay for a long long
time, and still only looked as though she were
asleep; for she was even now as white as snow,
and as red as blood, and as black as ebony.
At last a prince came and called at the dwarfs'
house; and he saw Snow-drop, and read what
was written in golden letters. Then he offered
the dwarfs money, and earnestly prayed them to
let him take her away; but they said, "We will
not part with her for all the gold in the world."
At last however they had pity on him, and gave
him the coffin: but the moment he lifted it up
to carry it home with him, the piece of apple fell
from between her lips, and Snow-drop awoke,
and said "Where am I?" And the prince answered, "Thou art safe with me." Then he told
her all that had happened, and said, "I love you
better than all the world: come with me to my
father's palace, and you shall be my wife."
And Snow-drop consented, and went home
with the prince; and every thing was pre-

pared with great pomp and splendour for their wedding.

To the feast was invited, among the rest, Snow-drop's old enemy the queen; and as she was dressing herself in fine rich clothes, she looked in the glass, and said,

> " Tell me, glass, tell me true !
> Of all the ladies in the land,
> Who is fairest ? tell me who ? "

And the glass answered,

> " Thou, lady, art loveliest *here*, I ween ;
> But lovelier far is the new-made queen."

When she heard this, she started with rage; but her envy and curiosity were so great, that she could not help setting out to see the bride. And when she arrived, and saw that it was no other than Snow-drop, who, as she thought, had been dead a long while, she choked with passion, and fell ill and died; but Snow-drop and the prince lived and reigned happily over that land many many years.

THE

ELVES AND THE SHOEMAKER.

THERE was once a shoemaker who worked very hard and was very honest; but still he could not earn enough to live upon, and at last all he had in the world was gone, except just leather enough to make one pair of shoes. Then he cut them all ready to make up the next day, meaning to get up early in the morning to work. His conscience was clear and his heart light amidst all his troubles; so he went peaceably to bed, left all his cares to heaven, and fell asleep. In the morning, after he had said his prayers, he set himself down to his work, when, to his great wonder, there stood the shoes, all ready made, upon the table. The good man knew not what to say or think of this strange event. He looked at the workmanship; there was not one false stitch in the whole job; and all was so neat and true, that it was a complete masterpiece.

That same day a customer came in, and the shoes pleased him so well that he willingly paid a price higher than usual for them; and the poor shoemaker with the money bought leather enough to make two pair more. In the evening he cut out the work, and went to bed early that he might get up and begin betimes next day: but he was saved all the trouble, for when he got up in the morning the work was finished ready to his hand. Presently in came buyers, who paid him handsomely for his goods, so that he bought leather enough for four pair more. He cut out the work again over night, and found it finished in the morning as before; and so it went on for some time: what was got ready in the evening was always done by day-break, and the good man soon became thriving and prosperous again.

One evening about Christmas time, as he and his wife were sitting over the fire chatting together, he said to her, " I should like to sit up and watch to-night, that we may see who it is that comes and does my work for me." The wife liked the thought; so they left a light burning, and hid themselves in the corner of the room behind a curtain that was hung up there, and watched what should happen.

As soon as it was midnight, there came two little naked dwarfs; and they sat themselves upon the shoemaker's bench, took up all the work that was cut out, and began to ply with their little fingers, stitching and rapping and tapping away at such a rate, that the shoemaker was all amazement, and could not take his eyes off for a moment. And on they went till the job was quite finished, and the shoes stood ready for use upon the table. This was long before day-break; and then they bustled away as quick as lightning.

The next day the wife said to the shoemaker, "These little wights have made us rich, and we ought to be thankful to them, and do them a good office in return. I am quite vexed to see them run about as they do; they have nothing upon their backs to keep off the cold. I'll tell you what, I will make each of them a shirt, and a coat and waistcoat, and a pair of pantaloons into the bargain; do you make each of them a little pair of shoes."

The thought pleased the good shoemaker very much; and one evening, when all the things were ready, they laid them on the table

instead of the work that they used to cut out,
and then went and hid themselves to watch
what the little elves would do. About midnight
they came in, and were going to sit down to their
work as usual; but when they saw the clothes
lying for them, they laughed and were greatly
delighted. Then they dressed themselves in the
twinkling of an eye, and danced and capered
and sprang about as merry as could be, till at
last they danced out at the door over the green;
and the shoemaker saw them no more: but
every thing went well with him from that time
forward, as long as he lived.

THE TURNIP.

THERE were two brothers who were both
soldiers; the one was rich and the other poor.
The poor man thought he would try to better
himself; so, pulling off his red coat, he became
a gardener, and dug his ground well, and
sowed turnips.

When the seed came up, there was one

plant bigger than all the rest; and it kept getting larger and larger, and seemed as if it would never cease growing; so that it might have been called the prince of turnips, for there never was such a one seen before, and never will again. At last it was so big that it filled a cart, and two oxen could hardly draw it; and the gardener knew not what in the world to do with it, nor whether it would be a blessing or a curse to him. One day he said to himself, " What shall I do with it? if I sell it, it will bring no more than another; and for eating, the little turnips are better than this; the best thing perhaps is to carry it and give it to the king as a mark of respect."

Then he yoked his oxen, and drew the turnip to the Court, and gave it to the king. " What a wonderful thing!" said the king; " I have seen many strange things, but such a monster as this I never saw. Where did you get the seed? or is it only your good luck? If so, you are a true child of fortune." " Ah, no !" answered the gardener, " I am no child of fortune; I am a poor soldier who never could get enough to live upon; so I laid aside my red coat, and

set to work, tilling the ground. I have a brother, who is rich, and your majesty knows him
well, and all the world knows him; but because I am poor, every body forgets me."

The king then took pity on him, and said,
" You shall be poor no longer. I will give you
so much that you shall be even richer than
your brother." Then he gave him gold and
lands and flocks, and made him so rich that
his brother's fortune could not at all be compared with his.

When the brother heard of all this, and how
a turnip had made the gardener so rich, he
envied him sorely, and bethought himself how
he could contrive to get the same good fortune
for himself. However, he determined to manage more cleverly than his brother, and got
together a rich present of gold and fine horses
for the king; and thought he must have a much
larger gift in return: for if his brother had received so much for only a turnip, what must
his present be worth?

The king took the gift very graciously, and
said he knew not what to give in return more
valuable and wonderful than the great turnip;

so the soldier was forced to put it into a cart, and drag it home with him. When he reached home, he knew not upon whom to vent his rage and spite; and at length wicked thoughts came into his head, and he resolved to kill his brother.

So he hired some villains to murder him; and having shown them where to lie in ambush, he went to his brother, and said, "Dear brother, I have found a hidden treasure; let us go and dig it up, and share it between us." The other had no suspicions of his roguery: so they went out together, and as they were travelling along, the murderers rushed out upon him, bound him, and were going to hang him on a tree.

But whilst they were getting all ready, they heard the trampling of a horse at a distance, which so frightened them that they pushed their prisoner neck and shoulders together into a sack, and swung him up by a cord to the tree, where they left him dangling, and ran away. Meantime he worked and worked away, till he made a hole large enough to put out his head.

When the horseman came up, he proved to be a student, a merry fellow, who was journeying along on his nag, and singing as he went. As soon as the man in the sack saw him passing under the tree, he cried out, " Good morning! good morning to thee, my friend!" The student looked about every where; and seeing no one, and not knowing where the voice came from, cried out, " Who calls me?"

Then the man in the tree answered, " Lift up thine eyes, for behold here I sit in the sack of wisdom; here have I, in a short time, learned great and wondrous things. Compared to this seat, all the learning of the schools is as empty air. A little longer, and I shall know all that man can know, and shall come forth wiser than the wisest of mankind. Here I discern the signs and motions of the heavens and the stars; the laws that control the winds; the number of the sands on the sea-shore; the healing of the sick; the virtues of all simples, of birds, and of precious stones. Wert thou but once here, my friend, thou wouldst feel and own the power of knowledge."

The student listened to all this and won-

dered much; at last he said, "Blessed be the
day and hour when I found you; cannot you
contrive to let me into the sack for a little
while?" Then the other answered, as if very
unwillingly, "A little space I may allow thee
to sit here, if thou wilt reward me well and
entreat me kindly; but thou must tarry yet an
hour below, till I have learnt some little matters that are yet unknown to me."

So the student sat himself down and waited
a while; but the time hung heavy upon him,
and he begged earnestly that he might ascend
forthwith, for his thirst of knowledge was great.
Then the other pretended to give way, and
said, "Thou must let the sack of wisdom descend, by untying yonder cord, and then thou
shalt enter." So the student let him down,
opened the sack, and set him free. "Now
then," cried he, "let me ascend quickly." As
he began to put himself into the sack heels
first, "Wait a while," said the gardener,
"that is not the way." Then he pushed him
in head first, tied up the sack, and soon swung
up the searcher after wisdom dangling in the
air. "How is it with thee, friend?" said he,

" dost thou not feel that wisdom comes unto thee? Rest there in peace, till thou art a wiser man than thou wert."

So saying, he trotted off on the student's nag, and left the poor fellow to gather wisdom till somebody should come and let him down.

―――――

OLD SULTAN.

A SHEPHERD had a faithful dog, called Sultan, who was grown very old, and had lost all his teeth. And one day when the shepherd and his wife were standing together before the house, the shepherd said, " I will shoot old Sultan to-morrow morning, for he is of no use now." But his wife said, " Pray let the poor faithful creature live; he has served us well a great many years, and we ought to give him a livelihood for the rest of his days." " But what can we do with him?" said the shepherd, " he has not a tooth in his head, and the thieves don't care for him at all; to be sure he has served us, but then he did it to earn his livelihood; to-morrow shall be his last day, depend upon it."

Poor Sultan, who was lying close by them, heard all that the shepherd and his wife said to one another, and was very much frightened to think to-morrow would be his last day; so in the evening he went to his good friend the wolf, who lived in the wood, and told him all his sorrows, and how his master meant to kill him in the morning. "Make yourself easy," said the wolf, "I will give you some good advice. Your master, you know, goes out every morning very early with his wife into the field; and they take their little child with them, and lay it down behind the hedge in the shade while they are at work. Now do you lie down close by the child, and pretend to be watching it, and I will come out of the wood and run away with it: you must run after me as fast as you can, and I will let it drop; then you may carry it back, and they will think you have saved their child, and will be so thankful to you that they will take care of you as long as you live." The dog liked this plan very well;

and accordingly so it was managed. The wolf ran with the child a little way; the shepherd and his wife screamed out; but Sultan soon overtook him, and carried the poor little thing back to his master and mistress. Then the shepherd patted him on the head, and said, " Old Sultan has saved our child from the wolf, and therefore he shall live and be well taken care of, and have plenty to eat. Wife, go home, and give him a good dinner, and let him have my old cushion to sleep on as long as he lives." So from this time forward Sultan had all that he could wish for.

Soon afterwards the wolf came and wished him joy, and said, " Now, my good fellow, you must tell no tales, but turn your head the other way when I want to taste one of the old shepherd's fine fat sheep." " No," said Sultan; " I will be true to my master." However, the wolf thought he was in joke, and came one night to get a dainty morsel. But Sultan had told his master what the wolf meant to do; so he laid wait for him behind the barn-door, and when the wolf was busy looking out for a good fat sheep, he had a stout cudgel laid about his back, that combed his locks for him finely.

Then the wolf was very angry, and called Sultan " an old rogue," and swore he would have his revenge. So the next morning the wolf sent the boar to challenge Sultan to come into the wood to fight the matter out. Now Sultan had no body he could ask to be his second but the shepherd's old three-legged cat; so he took her with him, and as the poor thing limped along with some trouble, she stuck up her tail straight in the air.

The wolf and the wild boar were first on the ground; and when they espied their enemies coming, and saw the cat's long tail standing straight in the air, they thought she was carrying a sword for Sultan to fight with; and every time she limped, they thought she was picking up a stone to throw at them; so they said they should not like this way of fighting, and the boar lay down behind a bush, and the wolf jumped up into a tree. Sultan and the cat soon came up, and looked about, and wondered that no one was there. The boar, however, had not quite hidden himself, for his ears stuck out of the bush; and when he shook one of them a little, the cat, seeing something move, and thinking it was a mouse, sprang upon it, and bit and scratched it, so that the boar jumped up and grunted, and ran away, roaring out, "Look up in the tree, there sits the one who is to blame." So they looked up, and espied the wolf sitting amongst the branches; and they called him a cowardly rascal, and would not suffer him to come down till he was heartily ashamed of himself, and had promised to be good friends again with old Sultan.

THE LADY AND THE LION.

A MERCHANT, who had three daughters, was once setting out upon a journey; but before he went he asked each daughter what gift he should bring back for her. The eldest wished for pearls; the second for jewels; but the third said, "Dear father, bring me a rose." Now it was no easy task to find a rose, for it was the middle of winter; yet, as she was the fairest daughter, and was very fond of flowers, her father said he would try what he could do. So he kissed all three, and bid them good bye. And when the time came for his return, he had bought pearls and jewels for the two eldest, but he had sought every where in vain for the rose; and when he went into any garden and inquired for such a thing, the people laughed at him, and asked him whether he thought roses grew in snow. This grieved him very much, for his third daughter was his dearest child; and as he was journeying home, thinking what he should bring her, he came to a fine castle; and around the castle was a garden, in half of which it appeared to be summer time, and in the other half winter. On one side the finest flowers were in full bloom, and on the other every thing looked desolate and buried in snow. "A lucky hit!" said he as he called to his servant, and told him to go to a beautiful bed of roses that was there, and bring him away one of the flowers. This done, they were riding away well pleased, when a fierce lion sprung up, and roared out, "Whoever dares to steal my roses shall be eaten up alive." Then the man said, "I knew not that the garden belonged to you; can nothing save my life?" "No!" said the lion, "nothing,

unless you promise to give me whatever meets
you first on your return home; if you agree to
this, I will give you your life, and the rose too
for your daughter." But the man was unwilling to do so, and said, " It may be my youngest daughter, who loves me most, and always
runs to meet me when I go home." Then the
servant was greatly frightened, and said, " It
may perhaps be only a cat or a dog." And at
last the man yielded with a heavy heart, and
took the rose; and promised the lion whatever
should meet him first on his return.

And as he came near home, it was his
youngest and dearest daughter that met him;
she came running and kissed him, and welcomed him home; and when she saw that he
had brought her the rose, she rejoiced still
more. But her father began to be very melancholy, and to weep, saying, "Alas! my dearest
child! I have bought this flower at a high price,
for I have promised to give you to a wild lion,
and when he has you, he will tear you in
pieces, and eat you." And he told her all
that had happened; and said she should not
go, let what would happen.

But she comforted him, and said, "Dear father, what you have promised must be fulfilled; I will go to the lion, and soothe him, perhaps he will let me return safe home again."

The next morning she asked the way she was to go, and took leave of her father, and went forth with a bold heart into the wood. But the lion was an enchanted prince, and by day he and all his court were lions, but in the evening they took their proper forms again. And when the lady came to the castle, he welcomed her so courteously that she consented to marry him. The wedding-feast was held, and they lived happily together a long time. The prince was only to be seen as soon as evening came, and then he held his court; but every morning he left his bride, and went away by himself, she knew not whither, till night came again.

After some time he said to her, "To-morrow there will be a great feast in your father's house, for your eldest sister is to be married; and, if you wish to go to visit her, my lions shall lead you thither." Then she rejoiced much at the thoughts of seeing her father once more, and set out with the lions; and every one

was overjoyed to see her, for they had thought
her dead long since.   But she told them how
happy she was; and stayed till the feast was
over, and then went back to the wood.

Her second sister was soon after married;
and when she was invited to the wedding, she
said to the prince,, "I will not go alone this time;
you must go with me." But he would not, and
said that would be a very hazardous thing, for
if the least ray of the torch light should fall upon
him, his enchantment would become still worse,
for he should be changed into a dove, and be
obliged to wander about the world for seven
long years.   However, she gave him no rest,
and said she would take care no light should fall
upon him.   So at last they set out together, and
took with them their little child; and she chose
a large hall with thick walls, for him to sit in
while the wedding torches were lighted; but
unluckily no one observed that there was a
crack in the door.   Then the wedding was held
with great pomp; but as the train came from
the church, and passed with the torches before
the hall, a very small ray of light fell upon the
prince.   In a moment he disappeared; and

when his wife came in, and looked for him, she found only a white dove. Then he said to her, "Seven years must I fly up and down over the face of the earth; but every now and then I will let fall a white feather, that shall show you the way I am going; follow it, and at last you may overtake and set me free."

This said, he flew out at the door, and she followed; and every now and then a white feather fell, and showed her the way she was to journey. Thus she went roving on through the wide world, and looked neither to the right hand nor to the left, nor took any rest for seven years. Then she began to rejoice, and thought to herself that the time was fast coming when all her troubles should cease: yet repose was still far off; for one day as she was travelling on, she missed the white feather, and when she lifted up her eyes she could no where see the dove. "Now," thought she to herself, "no human aid can be of use to me;" so she went to the sun, and said, "Thou shinest every where, on the mountain's top, and the valley's depth: hast thou any where seen my white dove?" "No," said the sun, "I have not seen it; but I will give thee a casket—open it when thy hour of need comes." So she thanked the sun, and went on her way till eventide; and when the moon arose, she cried unto it, and said, "Thou shinest through all the night, over field and grove: hast thou no where seen my white dove?" " No," said the moon, " I cannot help thee; but I will give thee an egg—break it when need comes." Then she thanked the moon, and went on till the night-wind blew; and she raised up her voice to it, and said, "Thou blowest through every tree and under every leaf: hast thou not seen the white dove?" " No," said the night-wind; "but I will ask three other winds; perhaps they have seen it." Then the east wind and the west wind came, and said they too had not seen it; but the south wind said, " I have seen the white dove; he has fled to the Red Sea, and is changed once more into a lion, for the seven years are passed away; and there he is fighting with a dragon, and the dragon is an enchanted princess, who seeks to separate him from you." Then the night-wind said, " I will give thee counsel: Go to the Red Sea; on the right shore stand many rods; number them, and when thou comest to the eleventh, break it off and smite the dragon with it; and so the lion will have the victory, and both of them will appear to you in their human forms. Then instantly set out with thy beloved prince, and journey home over sea and land."

So our poor wanderer went forth, and found all as the night-wind had said; and she plucked the eleventh rod, and smote the dragon, and immediately the lion became a prince and the dragon a princess again. But she forgot the counsel which the night-wind had given; and the false princess watched her opportunity, and took the prince by the arm, and carried him away.

Thus the unfortunate traveller was again forsaken and forlorn; but she took courage and said, " As far as the wind blows, and so long as the cock crows, I will journey on till I find him once again." She went on for a long long way, till at length she came to the castle whither the princess had carried the prince; and there was a feast prepared, and she heard that the wedding was about to be held. "Heaven aid me now!" said she; and she took the casket that the sun had given her, and found that within it lay a dress as dazzling as the sun itself. So she put it on, and went into the palace; and all the people gazed upon her; and the dress pleased the bride so much that she asked whether it was to be sold: " Not for gold and silver," answered she; " but for flesh and blood." The princess asked what she meant; and she said, " Let me speak with the bridegroom this night in his chamber, and I will give thee the dress." At last the princess agreed; but she told her chamberlain to give the prince a sleeping-draught, that he might not hear or see her. When evening came, and the prince had fallen asleep, she was led into his chamber, and she sat herself down at his feet and said, " I have followed thee seven years; I have been to the sun, the moon, and the night-wind, to seek thee; and at last I have helped thee to overcome the dragon. Wilt thou then forget me quite?" But the prince slept so soundly that her voice only passed over him, and seemed like the murmuring of the wind among the fir-trees.

Then she was led away, and forced to give up the golden dress; and when she saw that there was no help for her, she went out into a meadow and sat herself down and wept. But as she sat she bethought herself of the egg that the moon had given her; and when she broke it, there ran out a hen and twelve chickens of pure gold, that played about, and then nestled under the old one's wings, so as to form the most beautiful sight in the world. And she rose up, and drove them before her till the bride saw them from her window, and was so pleased that she came forth, and asked her if she would sell the brood. " Not for gold or silver; but for flesh and blood: let me again this evening speak with the bridegroom in his chamber."

Then the princess thought to betray her as before, and agreed to what she asked; but when the prince went to his chamber, he asked the chamberlain why the wind had murmured so in the night. And the chamberlain told him all; how he had given him a sleeping-draught, and a poor maiden had come and spoken to him in his chamber, and was to come again that night. Then the prince took care to throw away the sleeping-draught; and when she came and began again to tell him what woes had befallen her, and how faithful and true to him she had been, he knew his beloved wife's voice, and sprung up, and said, "You have awakened me as from a dream; for the strange princess had thrown a spell around me, so that I had altogether forgotten you: but heaven hath sent you to me in a lucky hour."

And they stole away out of the palace by night secretly, (for they feared the princess,) and journeyed home; and there they found their child, now grown comely and fair, and lived happily together to the end of their days.

THE JEW IN THE BUSH.

A FARMER had a faithful and diligent servant, who had worked hard for him three years, without having been paid any wages. At last it came into the man's head that he would not go on thus without pay any longer; so he went to his master, and said, " I have worked hard for you a long time, I will trust to you to give me what I deserve to have for my trouble." The farmer was a sad miser, and knew that his man was very simple-hearted; so he took out threepence, and gave him for every year's service a penny. The poor fellow thought it was a great deal of money to have, and said to himself, " Why should I work hard, and live here on bad fare any longer? I can now travel into the wide world, and make myself merry." With that he put his money into his purse, and set out, roaming over hill and valley.

As he jogged along over the fields, singing and dancing, a little dwarf met him, and asked him what made him so merry. " Why, what should make me down-hearted?" said he; " I am sound in health and rich in purse, what should I care for? I have saved up my three years' earnings, and have it all safe in my pocket." " How much may it come to?" said the little man. " Full threepence," replied the countryman. " I wish you would give them to me," said the other; " I am very poor." Then the man pitied him, and gave him all he had; and the little dwarf said in return, " As you have such a kind honest heart, I will grant you three wishes—one for each penny; so choose whatever you like." Then the countryman rejoiced at his good luck, and said, " I like many things better than money: first, I will have a bow that will bring down every thing I shoot at; secondly, a fiddle that will set every one dancing that hears me play upon it; and thirdly, I should like that every one should grant what I ask." The dwarf said he should have his three wishes; so he gave him the bow and fiddle, and went his way.

Our honest friend journeyed on his way too; and if he was merry before, he was now ten times more so. He had not gone far before he met an old Jew: close by them stood a tree, and on the topmost twig sat a thrush singing away most joyfully. " Oh, what a pretty bird!" said the Jew; I would give a great deal of money to have such a one." " If that's all," said the countryman, " I will soon bring it down." Then he took up his bow, and down fell the thrush into the bushes at the foot of the tree. The Jew crept into the bush to find it; but directly he had got into the middle, his companion took up his fiddle and played away, and the Jew began to dance and spring about, capering higher and higher in the air. The thorns soon began to tear his clothes till they all hung in rags about him, and he himself was all scratched and wounded, so that the blood ran down. " Oh, for heaven's sake ! " cried the Jew, " master! master! pray let the fiddle alone. What have I done to deserve this?" " Thou hast shaved many a poor soul close enough," said the other; " thou art only meeting thy reward:" so he played up another tune. Then the Jew began to beg and promise, and offered money for his liberty; but he did not come up to the musician's price for some time, and he danced him along brisker and brisker, and the Jew bid higher and higher, till at last he offered a round hundred of florins that he had in his purse, and had just gained by cheating some poor fellow. When the countryman saw so much money, he said, " I will agree to your proposal." So he took the purse, put up his fiddle, and travelled on, very well pleased with his bargain.

Meanwhile the Jew crept out of the bush half-naked and in a piteous plight, and began to ponder how he should take his revenge, and serve his late companion some trick. At last he went to the judge, and complained that a rascal had robbed him of his money, and

beaten him into the bargain; and that the fellow who did it carried a bow at his back and a
fiddle hung round his neck. Then the judge
sent out his officers to bring up the accused
wherever they should find him; and he was
soon caught and brought up to be tried.

The Jew began to tell his tale, and said he
had been robbed of his money. " No, you
gave it me for playing a tune to you," said the
countryman; but the judge told him that was
not likely, and cut the matter short by order-
ing him off to the gallows.

So away he was taken; but as he stood on
the steps he said, " My Lord Judge, may it
please you to grant me one last request."
" Any thing but thy life," replied the other.
" No," said he, " I do not ask my life; only
let me play upon my fiddle for the last time."
The Jew cried out, " Oh, no! no! for heaven's
sake don't listen to him! don't listen to him!"
But the judge said, " It is only for this once,
he will soon have done." The fact was, he
could not refuse the request, on account of the
dwarf's third gift.

Then the Jew said, " Bind me fast, bind me

fast, for pity's sake." But the countryman seized his fiddle, and struck up a tune, and at the first note judge, clerks, and jailer, were in motion; all began capering, and no one could hold the Jew. At the second note the hangman let his prisoner go, and danced also, and by the time he had played the first bar of the tune, all were dancing together—judge, court, and Jew, and all the people who had followed to look on. At first the thing was merry and pleasant enough; but when it had gone on a while, and there seemed to be no end of playing or dancing, they began to cry out, and beg him to leave off; but he stopt not a whit the more for their entreaties, till the judge not only gave him his life, but promised to return him the hundred florins.

Then he called to the Jew, and said, "Tell us now, you vagabond, where you got that gold, or I shall play on for your amusement only." "I stole it," said the Jew in the presence of all the people; "I acknowledge that I stole it, and that you earned it fairly." Then the countryman stopt his fiddle, and left the Jew to take his place at the gallows.

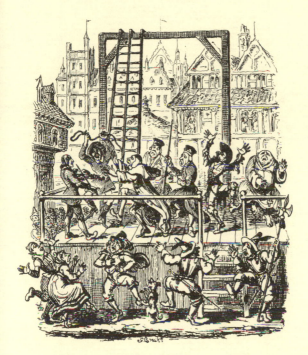

THE

KING of the GOLDEN MOUNTAIN.

A Certain merchant had two children, a son
and daughter, both very young, and scarcely
able to run alone. He had two richly laden
ships then making a voyage upon the seas, in
which he had embarked all his property, in
the hope of making great gains, when the news
came that they were lost. Thus from being a
rich man he became very poor, so that nothing
was left him but one small plot of land; and, to
relieve his mind a little of his trouble, he often
went out to walk there.

One day, as he was roving along, a little
rough-looking dwarf stood before him, and
asked him why he was so sorrowful, and what
it was that he took so deeply to heart. But
the merchant replied, " If you could do me any
good, I would tell you." " Who knows but I
may?" said the little man; "tell me what is the
matter, and perhaps I can be of some service."

I

Then the merchant told him how all his wealth was gone to the bottom of the sea, and how he had nothing left except that little plot of land. " Oh! trouble not yourself about that," said the dwarf; " only promise to bring me here, twelve years hence, whatever meets you first on your return home, and I will give you as much gold as you please." The merchant thought this was no great request; that it would most likely be his dog, or something of that sort, but forgot his little child: so he agreed to the bargain, and signed and sealed the engagement to do what was required.

But as he drew near home, his little boy was so pleased to see him, that he crept behind him and laid fast hold of his legs. Then the father started with fear, and saw what it was that he had bound himself to do; but as no gold was come, he consoled himself by thinking that it was only a joke that the dwarf was playing him.

About a month afterwards he went up stairs into an old lumber room to look for some old iron, that he might sell it and raise a little money; and there he saw a large pile of gold lying

on the floor. At the sight of this he was greatly
delighted, went into trade again, and became
a greater merchant than before.

Meantime his son grew up, and as the end
of the twelve years drew near, the merchant
became very anxious and thoughtful; so that
care and sorrow were written upon his face.
The son one day asked what was the matter:
but his father refused to tell for some time; at
last however he said that he had, without knowing it, sold him to a little ugly-looking dwarf
for a great quantity of gold; and that the twelve
years were coming round when he must per-
form his agreement. Then the son said, " Father, give yourself very little trouble about that;
depend upon it I shall be too much for the
little man."

When the time came, they went out together to the appointed place; and the son drew
a circle on the ground, and set himself and his
father in the middle. The little dwarf soon came,
and said to the merchant, " Have you brought
me what you promised?" The old man was
silent, but his son answered, " What do you
want here?" The dwarf said, " I come to

talk with your father, not with you." "You have deceived and betrayed my father," said the son; "give him up his bond." "No," replied the other, "I will not yield up my rights." Upon this a long dispute arose; and at last it was agreed that the son should be put into an open boat, that lay on the side of a piece of water hard by, and that the father should push him off with his own hand; so that he should be turned adrift. Then he took leave of his father, and set himself in the boat; and as it was pushed off it heaved, and fell on one side into the water: so the merchant thought that his son was lost, and went home very sorrowful.

But the boat went safely on, and did not sink; and the young man sat securely within, till at length it ran ashore upon an unknown land. As he jumped upon the shore, he saw before him a beautiful castle, but empty and desolate within, for it was enchanted. At last, however, he found a white snake in one of the chambers.

Now the white snake was an enchanted princess; and she rejoiced greatly to see him,

and said, " Art thou at last come to be my deliverer? Twelve long years have I waited for
thee, for thou alone canst save me. This night
twelve men will come: their faces will be
black, and they will be hung round with chains.
They will ask what thou dost here; but be silent, give no answer, and let them do what
they will—beat and torment thee. Suffer all,
only speak not a word, and at twelve o'clock
they must depart. The second night twelve
others will come: and the third night twenty-
four, who will even cut off thy head ; but at
the twelfth hour of that night their power is
gone, and I shall be free, and will come and
bring thee the water of life, and will wash thee
with it, and restore thee to life and health."
And all came to pass as she had said; the
merchant's son spoke not a word, and the
third night the princess appeared, and fell on
his neck and kissed him; joy and gladness
burst forth throughout the castle; the wedding
was celebrated, and he was king of the Golden
Mountain.

They lived together very happily, and the
queen had a son. Eight years had passed over

their heads when the king thought of his father: and his heart was moved, and he longed to see him once again. But the queen opposed his going, and said, " I know well that misfortunes will come." However, he gave her no rest till she consented. At his departure she presented him with a wishing-ring, and said, " Take this ring, and put it on your finger; whatever you wish it will bring you: only promise that you will not make use of it to bring me hence to your father's." Then he promised what she asked, and put the ring on his finger, and wished himself near the town where his father lived. He found himself at the gates in a moment; but the guards would not let him enter, because he was so strangely clad. So he went up to a neighbouring mountain where a shepherd dwelt, and borrowed his old frock, and thus passed unobserved into the town. When he came to his father's house, he said he was his son; but the merchant would not believe him, and said he had had but one son, who he knew was long since dead: and as he was only dressed like a poor shepherd, he would not even offer him any thing to eat. The king however

persisted that he was his son, and said, " Is there
no mark by which you would know if I am
really your son?" "Yes," observed his mother,
" our son has a mark like a raspberry under the
right arm." Then he showed them the mark, and
they were satisfied that what he had said was
true. He next told them how he was king of
the Golden Mountain, and was married to a
princess, and had a son seven years old. But
the merchant said, " That can never be true; he
must be a fine king truly who travels about in
a shepherd's frock." At this the son was very
angry; and, forgetting his promise, turned his
ring, and wished for his queen and son. In an
instant they stood before him; but the queen
wept, and said he had broken his word, and
misfortune would follow. He did all he could
to soothe her, and she at last appeared to be
appeased; but she was not so in reality, and
only meditated how she should take her revenge.

One day he took her to walk with him out
of the town, and showed her the spot where
the boat was turned adrift upon the wide waters. Then he sat himself down, and said, " I

am very much tired; sit by me, I will rest my head in your lap, and sleep a while." As soon as he had fallen asleep, however, she drew the ring from his finger, and crept softly away, and wished herself and her son at home in their kingdom. And when the king awoke, he found himself alone, and saw that the ring was gone from his finger. "I can never return to my father's house," said he; "they would say I am a sorcerer: I will journey forth into the world till I come again to my kingdom."

So saying, he set out and travelled till he came to a mountain, where three giants were sharing their inheritance; and as they saw him pass, they cried out and said "Little men have sharp wits; he shall divide the inheritance between us." Now it consisted of a sword that cut off an enemy's head whenever the wearer gave the words "Heads off!"—a cloak that made the owner invisible, or gave him any form he pleased; and a pair of boots that transported the person who put them on wherever he wished. The king said they must first let him try these wonderful things, that he might know how to set a value upon them. Then they gave him the cloak, and he wished himself a fly, and in a moment he was a fly. " The cloak is very well," said he; " now give me the sword." " No," said they, " not unless you promise not to say ' Heads off ! ' for if you do, we are all dead men." So they gave it him on condition that he tried its virtue only on a tree. He next asked for the boots also; and the moment he had all three in his possession he wished himself at the Golden Mountain ; and there he was in an instant. So the giants were left behind with no inheritance to divide or quarrel about.

As he came near to thé castle he heard the sound of merry music; and the people around told him that his queen was about to celebrate her marriage with another prince. Then he threw his cloak around him, and passed through the castle, and placed himself by the side of his queen, where no one saw him. But when any thing to eat was put upon her plate, he took it away and ate it himself; and when a glass of wine was handed to her, he took and drank it: and thus, though they kept on serving her with meat and drink, her plate continued always empty.

Upon this, fear and remorse came over her, and she went into her chamber and wept; and he followed her there. "Alas!" said she to herself, "did not my deliverer come? why then doth enchantment still surround me?"

"Thou traitress!" said he, "thy deliverer indeed came, and now is near thee: has he deserved this of thee?" And he went out and dismissed the company, and said the wedding was at an end, for that he was returned to his kingdom: but the princes and nobles and counsellors mocked at him. However, he would enter into no parley with them, but only demanded whether they would depart in peace, or not. Then they turned and tried to seize him; but he drew his sword, and, with a word, the traitors' heads fell before him; and he was once more king of the Golden Mountain.

THE GOLDEN GOOSE.

THERE was a man who had three sons. The youngest was called Dummling, and was on all

occasions despised and ill-treated by the whole family. It happened that the eldest took it into his head one day to go into the wood to cut fuel; and his mother gave him a delicious pasty and a bottle of wine to take with him, that he might refresh himself at his work. As he went into the wood, a little old man bid him good day, and said, " Give me a little piece of meat from your plate, and a little wine out of your bottle; I am very hungry and thirsty." But this clever young man said, " Give you my meat and wine! No, I thank you; I should not have enough left for myself:" and away he went. He soon began to cut down a tree; but he had not worked long before he missed his stroke, and cut himself, and was obliged to go home to have the wound dressed. Now it was the little old man that caused him this mischief.

Next went out the second son to work; and his mother gave him too a pasty and a bottle of wine. And the same little old man met him also, and asked him for something to eat and drink. But he too thought himself vastly clever, and said, " Whatever you get, I shall

lose; so go your way!" The little man took
care that he should have his reward; and the
second stroke that he aimed against a tree, hit
him on the leg; so that he too was forced to
go home.

Then Dummling said, " Father, I should
like to go and cut wood too." But his father
answered, " Your brothers have both lamed
themselves; you had better stay at home, for
you know nothing of the business." But
Dummling was very pressing; and at last his
father said, "Go your way; you will be wiser
when you have suffered for your folly." And
his mother gave him only some dry bread, and
a bottle of sour beer : but when he went into
the wood, he met the little old man, who said,
"Give me some meat and drink, for I am very
hungry and thirsty." Dummling said, "I have
only dry bread and sour beer; if that will suit
you, we will sit down and eat it together." So
they sat down; and when the lad pulled out
his bread, behold it was turned into a capital
pasty, and his sour beer became delightful wine.
They ate and drank heartily; and when they
had done, the little man said, " As you have a

kind heart, and have been willing to share every thing with me, I will send a blessing upon you. There stands an old tree; cut it down, and you will find something at the root." Then he took his leave, and went his way.

Dummling set to work, and cut down the tree; and when it fell, he found in a hollow under the roots a goose with feathers of pure gold. He took it up, and went on to an inn, where he proposed to sleep for the night. The landlord had three daughters; and when they saw the goose, they were very curious to examine what this wonderful bird could be, and wished very much to pluck one of the feathers out of its tail. At last the eldest said, "I must and will have a feather." So she waited till his back was turned, and then seized the goose by the wing; but to her great surprise there she stuck, for neither hand nor finger could she get away again. Presently in came the second sister, and thought to have a feather too; but the moment she touched her sister, there she too hung fast. At last came the third, and wanted a feather; but the other two cried out, "Keep away! for heaven's sake, keep away!" However, she did not understand what they meant. "If they are there," thought she, "I may as well be there too." So she went up to them; but the moment she touched her sisters she stuck fast, and hung to the goose as they did. And so they kept company with the goose all night.

The next morning Dummling carried off the goose under his arm; and took no notice of the three girls, but went out with them sticking fast behind; and wherever he travelled, they too were obliged to follow, whether they would or no, as fast as their legs could carry them.

In the middle of a field the parson met them; and when he saw the train, he said, "Are you not ashamed of yourselves, you bold girls, to run after the young man in that way over the fields? is that proper behaviour?" Then he took the youngest by the hand to lead her away; but the moment he touched her he too hung fast, and followed in the train. Presently up came the clerk; and when he saw his master the parson running after the three girls, he wondered greatly, and said, "Hollo! hollo! your reverence! whither so fast? there is a christen-

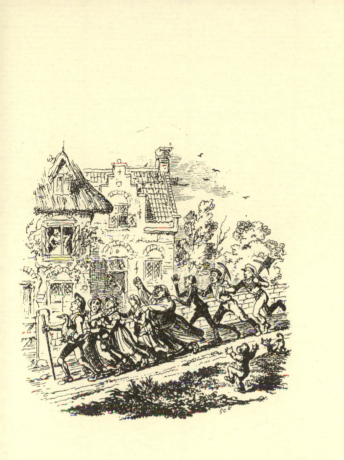

ing to-day." Then he ran up, and took him
by the gown, and in a moment he was fast too.
As the five were thus trudging along, one behind another, they met two labourers with
their mattocks coming from work; and the
parson cried out to them to set him free. But
scarcely had they touched him, when they too
fell into the ranks, and so made seven, all running after Dummling and his goose.

At last they arrived at a city, where reigned
a king who had an only daughter. The princess was of so thoughtful and serious a turn of
mind that no one could make her laugh; and
the king had proclaimed to all the world, that
whoever could make her laugh should have
her for his wife. When the young man heard
this, he went to her with his goose and all its
train; and as soon as she saw the seven all
hanging together, and running about, treading
on each other's heels, she could not help bursting into a long and loud laugh. Then Dummling claimed her for his wife; the wedding was
celebrated, and he was heir to the kingdom,
and lived long and happily with his wife.

Mrs. FOX.

THERE was once a sly old fox with nine tails, who was very curious to know whether his wife was true to him: so he stretched himself out under a bench, and pretended to be as dead as a mouse.

Then Mrs. Fox went up into her own room and locked the door: but her maid, the cat, sat at the kitchen fire cooking; and soon after it became known that the old fox was dead, some one knocked at the door, saying,

" Miss Pussy! Miss Pussy! how fare you to-day?
Are you sleeping or watching the time away?"

Then the cat went and opened the door, and there stood a young fox; so she said to him,

" No, no, Master Fox, I don't sleep in the day,
I'm making some capital white wine whey.
Will your honour be pleased to dinner to stay?"

" No, I thank you," said the fox; " but how is poor Mrs. Fox?" Then the cat answered,

" She sits all alone in her chamber up stairs,
And bewails her misfortune with floods of tears:
She weeps till her beautiful eyes are red;
For, alas! alas! Mr. Fox is dead."

" Go to her," said the other, " and say that there is a young fox come, who wishes to marry her."

Then up went the cat,—trippety trap,
And knocked at the door,—tippety tap;
" Is good Mrs. Fox within ? " said she.
" Alas ! my dear, what want you with me?"
" There waits a suitor below at the gate."

Then said Mrs. Fox,

" How looks he, my dear ? is he tall and straight ?
Has he nine good tails ? There must be nine,
Or he never shall be a suitor of mine."

" Ah !" said the cat, " he has but one."
" Then I will never have him," answered Mrs. Fox.

So the cat went down, and sent this suitor about his business. Soon after, some one else knocked at the door; it was another fox that had two tails, but he was not better welcomed than the first. After this came several others, till at last one came that had really nine tails just like the old fox.

When the widow heard this, she jumped up and said,

" Now, Pussy, my dear, open windows and doors,
 And bid all our friends at our wedding to meet;
 And as for that nasty old master of ours,
 Throw him out of the window, Puss, into the street."

But when the wedding feast was all ready,
up sprung the old gentleman on a sudden, and
taking a club drove the whole company, together with Mrs. Fox, out of doors.

After some time, however, the old fox really
died; and soon afterwards a wolf came to pay
his respects, and knocked at the door.

Wolf. Good day, Mrs. Cat, with your whiskers so
   trim;
 How comes it you're sitting alone so prim?
 What's that you are cooking so nicely, I pray?
Cat. O, that's bread and milk for my dinner to-day.
 Will your worship be pleased to stay and dine,
 Or shall I fetch you a glass of wine?

" No, I thank you: Mrs. Fox is not at home,
I suppose?"

Cat. She sits all alone,
 Her griefs to bemoan;
 For, alas! alas! Mr. Fox is gone.

Wolf. Ah ! dear Mrs. Puss ! that's a loss indeed :
　　D'ye think she'd take *me* for a hnsband instead?
Cat. "Indeed, Mr. Wolf, I don't know but she may;
　　If you'll sit down a moment, I'll step up and see."
　　So she gave him a chair, and shaking her ears,
　　She very obligingly tripped it up stairs.
　　She knocked at the door with the rings on her toes,
　　And said, "Mrs. Fox, you're within, I suppose?"
"O yes," said the widow, "pray come in, my dear,
　　And tell me whose voice in the kitchen I hear."
"It's a wolf," said the cat, "with a nice smooth skin,
　　Who was passing this way, and just stepped in
　　To see (as old Mr. Fox is dead)
　　If you like to take him for a husband instead."

"But," said Mrs. Fox, "has he red feet and
a sharp snout?" "No," said the cat. "Then
he won't do for me." Soon after the wolf was
sent about his business, there came a dog,
then a goat, and after that a bear, a lion, and
all the beasts, one after another. But they all
wanted something that old Mr. Fox had, and
the cat was ordered to send them all away.
At last came a young fox, and Mrs. Fox said,
"Has he four red feet and a sharp snout?"
"Yes," said the cat.

"Then, Puss, make the parlour look clean and neat,
  And throw the old gentleman into the street;
  A stupid old rascal! I'm glad that he's dead,
  Now I've got such a charming young fox instead."
So the wedding was held, and the merry bells rung,
And the friends and relations they danced and they
    sung,
And feasted and drank, I can't tell how long.

<hr>

HANSEL AND GRETTEL.

Hansel one day took his sister Grettel by
the hand, and said "Since our poor mother
died we have had no happy days; for our new
mother beats us all day long, and when we
go near her, she pushes us away. We have
nothing but hard crusts to eat; and the little
dog that lies by the fire is better off than we;
for he sometimes has a nice piece of meat
thrown to him. Heaven have mercy upon
us! O if our poor mother knew how we are
used! Come, we will go and travel over the
wide world." They went the whole day walk-

ing over the fields, till in the evening they
came to a great wood; and then they were so
tired and hungry that they sat down in a hollow tree and went to sleep.

In the morning when they awoke, the sun
had risen high above the trees, and shone
warm upon the hollow tree. Then Hansel
said, " Sister, I am very thirsty; if I could find
a brook, I would go and drink, and fetch you
some water too. Listen, I think I hear the
sound of one." Then Hansel rose up and took
Grettel by the hand and went in search of the
brook. But their cruel step-mother was a
fairy, and had followed them into the wood to
work them mischief: and when they had found
a brook that ran sparkling over the pebbles,
Hansel wanted to drink; but Grettel thought
she heard the brook, as it babbled along, say
" Whoever drinks here will be turned into a
tiger." Then she cried out, " Ah, brother! do
not drink, or you will be turned into a wild
beast and tear me to pieces." Then Hansel
yielded, although he was parched with thirst.
" I will wait," said he, " for the next brook."
But when they came to the next, Grettel

listened again, and thought she heard " Whoever drinks here will become a wolf." Then she cried out " Brother, brother, do not drink, or you will become a wolf and eat me." So he did not drink, but said, " I will wait for the next brook; there I must drink, say what you will, I am so thirsty."

As they came to the third brook, Grettel listened, and heard " Whoever drinks here will become a fawn." " Ah brother !" said she, " do not drink, or you will be turned into a fawn and run away from me." But Hansel had already stooped down upon his knees, and the moment he put his lips into the water he was turned into a fawn.

Grettel wept bitterly over the poor creature, and the tears too rolled down his eyes as he laid himself beside her. Then she said, " Rest in peace, dear fawn, I will never never leave thee." So she took off her golden necklace and put it round his neck, and plucked some rushes and plaited them into a soft string to fasten to it; and led the poor little thing by her side further into the wood.

After they had travelled a long way, they

came at last to a little cottage; and Grettel, having looked in and seen that it was quite empty, thought to herself, " We can stay and live here." Then she went and gathered leaves and moss to make a soft bed for the fawn: and every morning she went out and plucked nuts, roots, and berries for herself, and sweet shrubs and tender grass for her companion; and it ate out of her hand, and was pleased, and played and frisked about her. In the evening, when Grettel was tired, and had said her prayers, she laid her head upon the fawn for her pillow, and slept: and if poor Hansel could but have his right form again, they thought they should lead a very happy life.

They lived thus a long while in the wood by themselves, till it chanced that the king of that country came to hold a great hunt there. And when the fawn heard all around the echoing of the horns, and the baying of the dogs, and the merry shouts of the huntsmen, he wished very much to go and see what was going on. " Ah sister! sister!" said he, " let me go out into the wood, I can stay no longer." And he begged so long, that she at last agreed to let him go.

" But," said she, " be sure to come to me in the evening; I shall shut up the door to keep out those wild huntsmen; and if you tap at it, and say ' Sister, let me in,' I shall know you; but if you don't speak, I shall keep the door fast." Then away sprang the fawn, and frisked and bounded along in the open air. The king and his huntsmen saw the beautiful creature, and followed but could not overtake him; for when they thought they were sure of their prize, he sprung over the bushes and was out of sight in a moment.

As it grew dark he came running home to the hut, and tapped, and said " Sister, sister, let me in." Then she opened the little door, and in he jumped and slept soundly all night on his soft bed.

Next morning the hunt began again; and when he heard the huntsmen's horns, he said " Sister, open the door for me, I must go again." Then she let him out, and said " Come back in the evening, and remember what you are to say." When the king and the huntsmen saw the fawn with the golden collar again, they gave him chase; but he was too quick for them. The chase lasted the whole day; but at last the huntsmen nearly surrounded him, and one of them wounded him in the foot, so that he became sadly lame and could hardly crawl home. The man who had wounded him followed close behind, and hid himself, and heard the little fawn say, " Sister, sister, let me in:" upon which the door opened and soon shut again. The huntsman marked all well, and went to the king and told him what he had seen and heard; then the king said, " To-morrow we will have another chase."

Grettel was very much frightened when she saw that her dear little fawn was wounded; but she washed the blood away and put some healing herbs on it, and said, " Now go to bed, dear fawn, and you will soon be well again." The wound was so small, that in the morning there was nothing to be seen of it; and when the horn blew, the little creature said " I can't stay here, I must go and look on; I will take care that none of them shall catch me." But Grettel said, " I am sure they will kill you this time, I will not let you go." " I shall

K

die of vexation," answered he, "if you keep me here; when I hear the horns, I feel as if I could fly." Then Grettel was forced to let him go; so she opened the door with a heavy heart, and he bounded out gaily into the wood.

When the king saw him, he said to his huntsman, "Now chase him all day long till you catch him; but let none of you do him any harm." The sun set, however, without their being able to overtake him, and the king called away the huntsmen, and said to the one who had watched, "Now come and show me the little hut." So they went to the door and tapped, and said, "Sister, sister, let me in." Then the door opened and the king went in, and there stood a maiden more lovely than any he had ever seen. Grettel was frightened to see that it was not her fawn, but a king with a golden crown, that was come into her hut: however, he spoke kindly to her, and took her hand, and said, "Will you come with me to my castle and be my wife?" "Yes," said the maiden; "but my fawn must go with me, I cannot part with that." "Well," said the king, "he shall come and live with you all your life, and want for nothing." Just at that moment in sprung the little fawn: and his sister tied the string to his neck, and they left the hut in the wood together.

Then the king took Grettel to his palace, and celebrated the marriage in great state. And she told the king all her story; and he sent for the fairy and punished her: and the fawn was changed into Hansel again, and he and his sister loved one another, and lived happily together all their days.

THE GIANT WITH THE THREE GOLDEN HAIRS.

There was once a poor man who had an only son born to him. The child was born under a lucky star; and those who told his fortune said that in his fourteenth year he would marry the king's daughter. It so happened that the king of that land, soon after the child's birth, passed through the village in disguise, and asked whether there was any news. "Yes," said the people, " a child has just been born, that they say is to be a lucky one, and when he is fourteen years old, he is fated to marry the king's daughter." This did not please the king; so he went to the poor child's parents and asked them whether they would sell him their son? " No," said they; but the stranger begged very hard and offered a great deal of money, and they had scarcely bread to eat; so at last they consented, thinking to themselves, he is a luck's child, he can come to no harm.

The king took the child, put it into a box, and rode away; but when he came to a deep stream, he threw it into the current, and said to himself, " That young gentleman will never be my daughter's husband." The box however floated down the stream; some kind spirit watched over it so that no water reached the child, and at last about two miles from the king's capital it stopt at the dam of a mill. The miller soon saw it, and took a long pole, and drew it towards the shore, and finding it heavy, thought there was gold inside; but when he opened it, he found a pretty little boy, that smiled upon him merrily. Now the miller and his wife had no children, snd therefore rejoiced to see their prize, saying, " Heaven has sent it to us; " so they treated it very kindly, and brought it up with such care that every one admired and loved it.

About thirteen years passed over their heads, when the king came by accident to the mill, and asked the miller if that was his son. " No," said he, " I found him when a babe in a box in the mill-dam." " How long ago?" asked the king. " Some thirteen years," replied the miller. " He is a fine fellow," said the king, " can you spare him to carry a letter to the queen? it will oblige me very much, and I will give him two pieces of gold for his trouble." "As your majesty pleases," answered the miller.

Now the king had soon guessed that this was the child whom he had tried to drown; and he wrote a letter by him to the queen, saying, " As soon as the bearer of this arrives, let him be killed and immediately buried, so that all may be over before I return."

The young man set out with this letter, but missed his way, and came in the evening to a dark wood. Through the gloom he perceived a light at a distance, towards which he directed his course, and found that it proceeded from a little cottage. There was no one within except an old woman, who was frightened at seeing him, and said, " Why do you come hither, and whither are you going?" " I am going to the queen, to whom I was to have delivered a letter; but I have lost my way, and shall be glad if you will give me a night's rest." " You are very unlucky," said she, " for this is a robbers' hut, and if the band returns while you are here it may be worse for you." " I am so tired, however," replied he, " that I must take my chance, for I can go no further;" so he laid the letter on the table, stretched himself out upon a bench, and fell asleep.

When the robbers came home and saw him, they asked the old woman who the strange lad was. " I have given him shelter for charity," said she; " he had a letter to carry to the queen, and lost his way." The robbers took up the letter, broke it open and read the directions which it contained to murder the bearer. Then their leader tore it, and wrote a fresh one desiring the queen, as soon as the young man

arrived, to marry him to the king's daughter.
Meantime they let him sleep on till morning
broke, and then showed him the right way to
the queen's palace; where, as soon as she had
read the letter, she had all possible prepara-
tions made for the wedding; and as the young
man was very beautiful, the princess took him
willingly for her husband.

After a while the king returned; and when
he saw the prediction fulfilled, and that this
child of fortune was, notwithstanding all his
cunning, married to his daughter, he inquired
eagerly how this had happened, and what were
the orders which he had given. " Dear husband," said the queen, " here is your letter,
read it for yourself." The king took it, and
seeing that an exchange had been made, asked
his son-in-law what he had done with the
letter which he had given him to carry. " I
know nothing of it," answered he; " it must
have been taken away in the night while I
slept." Then the king was very wroth, and
said, " No man shall have my daughter who
does not descend into the wonderful cave and
bring me three golden hairs from the head of

the giant king who reigns there; do this and
you shall have my consent." " I will soon manage that," said the youth;—so he took leave
of his wife and set out on his journey.

At the first city that he came to, the guard
of the gate stopt him, and asked what trade he
followed, and what he knew. " I know every
thing," said he. " If that be so," replied they,
" you are just the man we want; be so good
as to tell us why our fountain in the market-
place is dry and will give no water; find out
the cause of that, and we will give you two
asses loaded with gold." " With all my
heart," said he, " when I come back."

Then he journeyed on and came to another
city, and there the guard also asked him what
trade he followed, and what he understood.
" I know every thing," answered he. " Then
pray do us a piece of service," said they, " tell
us why a tree which used to bear us golden apples, now does not even produce a leaf." "Most
willingly," answered he, " as I come back."

At last his way led him to the side of a great
lake of water over which he must pass. The
ferryman soon began to ask, as the others had

done, what was his trade, and what he knew. " Every thing," said he. " Then," said the other, " pray inform me why I am bound for ever to ferry over this water, and have never been able to get my liberty; I will reward you handsomely." " I will tell you all about it," said the young man, " as I come home."

When he had passed the water, he came to the wonderful cave, which looked terribly black and gloomy. But the wizard king was not at home, and his grandmother sat at the door in her easy chair. " What do you seek?" said she. " Three golden hairs from the giant's head," answered he. " You run a great risk," said she, " when he returns home; yet I will try what I can do for you." Then she changed him into an ant, and told him to hide himself in the folds of her cloak. " Very well," said he: " but I want also to know why the city fountain is dry, why the tree that bore golden apples is now leafless, and what it is that binds the ferryman to his post." " Those are three puzzling questions," said the old dame; " but lie quiet and listen to what the giant says when I pull the golden hairs."

Presently night set in and the old gentleman returned home. As soon as he entered
he began to snuff up the air, and cried, " All
is not right here: I smell man's flesh." Then
he searched all round in vain, and the old
dame scolded, and said " Why should you
turn every thing topsy-turvy? I have just set
all in order." Upon this he laid his head in
her lap and soon fell asleep. As soon as he
began to snore, she seized one of the golden
hairs and pulled it out. " Mercy ! " cried he,
starting up, " what are you about?" " I had
a dream that disturbed me," said she, " and in
my trouble I seized your hair: I dreamt that
the fountain in the market-place of the city
was become dry and would give no water;
what can be the cause?" " Ah ! if they could
find that out, they would be glad," said the
giant: " under a stone in the fountain sits a
toad; when they kill him, it will flow again."

This said, he fell asleep, and the old lady
pulled out another hair. " What would you
be at?" cried he in a rage. " Don't be angry,"
said she, " I did it in my sleep; I dreamt that
in a great kingdom there was a beautiful tree

that used to bear golden apples, and now has not even a leaf upon it; what is the reason of that?" "Aha!" said the giant, "they would like very well to know that secret: at the root of the tree a mouse is gnawing; if they were to kill him, the tree would bear golden apples again; if not, it will soon die. Now let me sleep in peace; if you wake me again, you shall rue it."

Then he fell once more asleep; and when she heard him snore she pulled out the third golden hair, and the giant jumped up and threatened her sorely; but she soothed him, and said, "It was a strange dream: methought I saw a ferryman who was fated to ply backwards and forwards over a lake, and could never be set at liberty; what is the charm that binds him?" "A silly fool!" said the giant: "If he were to give the rudder into the hand of any passenger, he would find himself at liberty, and the other would be obliged to take his place. Now let me sleep."

In the morning the giant arose and went out; and the old woman gave the young man the three golden hairs, reminded him of the answers to his three questions, and sent him on his way.

He soon came to the ferryman, who knew him again, and asked for the answer which he had promised him. "Ferry me over first," said he, "and then I will tell you." When the boat arrived on the other side, he told him to give the rudder to any of his passengers, and then he might run away as soon as he pleased. The next place he came to was the city where the barren tree stood: "Kill the mouse," said he, "that gnaws the root, and you will have golden apples again." They gave him a rich present, and he journeyed on to the city where the fountain had dried up, and the guard demanded his answer to their question. So he told them how to cure the mischief, and they thanked him and gave him the two asses laden with gold.

And now at last this child of fortune reached home, and his wife rejoiced greatly to see him, and to hear how well every thing had gone with him. He gave the three golden hairs to the king, who could no longer raise any objection to him, and when he saw all the treasure, cried out in a transport of joy, " Dear son, where did you find all this gold ?" " By the side of a lake," said the youth, " where there is plenty more to be had." " Pray, tell me," said the king, " that I may go and get some too." " As much as you please," replied the other; " you will see the ferryman on the lake, let him carry you across, and there you will see gold as plentiful as sand upon the shore."

Away went the greedy king; and when he came to the lake, he beckoned to the ferryman, who took him into his boat, and as soon as he was there gave the rudder into his hand, and sprung ashore, leaving the old king to ferry away as a reward for his sins.

" And is his majesty plying there to this day?" You may be sure of that, for nobody will trouble himself to take the rudder out of his hands.

THE FROG-PRINCE.

ONE fine evening a young princess went into a wood, and sat down by the side of a cool spring of water.   She had a golden ball in her hand, which was her favourite play-thing, and she amused herself with tossing it into the air and catching it again as it fell. After a time she threw it up so high that when she stretched out her hand to catch it, the ball bounded away and rolled along upon the ground, till at last it fell into the spring. The princess looked into the spring after her ball; but it was very deep, so deep that she could not see the bottom of it. Then she began to lament her loss, and said, " Alas! if I could only get my ball again, I would give all my fine clothes and jewels, and every thing that I have in the world." Whilst she was speaking a frog put its head out of the water, and said " Princess, why do you weep so bitterly?" " Alas!" said she, " what can you do for me, you nasty frog? My golden ball has fallen into the spring." The frog said, " I want not your pearls and jewels and fine clothes; but if you will love me and let me live with you, and eat from your little golden plate, and sleep upon your little bed, I will bring you your ball again." " What nonsense," thought the princess, " this silly frog is talking! He can never get out of the well: however, he may be able to get my ball for me; and there- fore I will promise him what he asks." So she said to the frog, " Well, if you will bring me my ball, I promise to do all you require." Then the frog put his head down, and dived deep under the water; and after a little while he came up again with the ball in his mouth, and threw it on the ground. As soon as the young princess saw her ball, she ran to pick it up, and was so overjoyed to have it in her hand again, that she never thought of the frog, but ran home with it as fast as she could. The frog called after her, " Stay, princess, and take me with you as you promised;" but she did not stop to hear a word.

The next day, just as the princess had sat down to dinner, she heard a strange noise, tap-tap, as if somebody was coming up the mar-ble-staircase; and soon afterwards something knocked gently at the door, and said,

" Open the door, my princess dear,
Open the door to thy true love here !
And mind the words that thou and I said
By the fountain cool in the greenwood shade."

Then the princess ran to the door and opened it, and there she saw the frog, whom she had quite forgotten; she was terribly frightened, and shutting the door as fast as she could, came back to her seat. The king her father asked her what had frightened her. " There is a nasty frog," said she, " at the door, who lifted my ball out of the spring this morning : I promised him that he should live with me here, thinking that he could never get out of the spring; but there he is at the door and wants to come in ! " While she was speaking the frog knocked again at the door, and said,

" Open the door, my princess dear,
Open the door to thy true love here !
And mind the words that thou and I said
By the fountain cool in the greenwood shade."

The king said to the young princess, " As you have made a promise, you must keep it; so go and let him in." She did so, and the frog hopped into the room, and came up close to the table. " Pray lift me upon a chair," said he to the princess, " and let me sit next to you." As soon as she had done this, the frog said " Put your plate closer to me that I may eat out of it." This she did, and when he had eaten as much as he could, he said " Now I am tired ; carry me up stairs and put me into your little bed." And the princess took him up in her hand and put him upon the pillow of her own little bed, where he slept all night long. As soon as it was light he jumped up, hopped down stairs, and went out of the house. "Now," thought the princess, "he is gone, and I shall be troubled with him no more."

But she was mistaken; for when night came again, she heard the same tapping at the door, and when she opened it, the frog came in and slept upon her pillow as before till the morning broke; and the third night he did the same: but when the princess awoke on the following morning, she was astonished to see, instead of the frog, a handsome prince gazing on her with the most beautiful eyes that ever were seen, and standing at the head of her bed.

He told her that he had been enchanted by a malicious fairy, who had changed him into the form of a frog, in which he was fated to remain till some princess should take him out of the spring and let him sleep upon her bed for three nights. "You," said the prince, "have broken this cruel charm, and now I have nothing to wish for but that you should go with me into my father's kingdom, where I will marry you, and love you as long as you live."

The young princess, you may be sure, was not long in giving her consent; and as they spoke, a splendid carriage drove up with eight beautiful horses decked with plumes of feathers and golden harness, and behind rode the prince's servant, the faithful Henry, who had bewailed the misfortune of his dear master so long and bitterly that his heart had well nigh burst. Then all set out full of joy for the Prince's kingdom; where they arrived safely, and lived happily a great many years.

THE FOX AND THE HORSE.

A FARMER had a horse that had been an excellent faithful servant to him: but he was now grown too old to work : so the farmer would give him nothing more to eat, and said " I want you no longer, so take yourself off out of my stable : I shall not take you back again until you are stronger than a lion." Then he opened the door and turned him adrift.

The poor horse was very melancholy, and wandered up and down in the wood, seeking some little shelter from the cold wind and rain.

Presently a fox met him: "What's the matter, my friend?" said he, "why do you hang down your head and look so lonely and woe-begone?" "Ah!" replied the horse, "justice and avarice never dwell in one house; my master has forgotten all that I have done for him so many years, and because I can no longer work he has turned me adrift, and says unless I become stronger than a lion he will not take me back again; what chance can I have of that? he knows I have none, or he would not talk so."

However, the fox bid him be of good cheer, and said, "I will help you; lie down there, stretch yourself out quite stiff, and pretend to be dead." The horse did as he was told, and the fox went straight to the lion who lived in a cave close by, and said to him, "A little way off lies a dead horse; come with me and you may make an excellent meal of his carcase." The lion was greatly pleased, and set off immediately: and when they came to the horse, the fox said "You will not be able to eat him comfortably here; I'll tell you what—I will tie you fast to his tail, and then you can draw him to your den, aud eat him at your leisure."

This advice pleased the lion, so he laid himself down quietly for the fox to make him fast to the horse. But the fox managed to tie his legs together, and bound all so hard and fast that with all his strength he could not set himself free. When the work was done, the fox clapped the horse on the shoulder, and said " Jip ! Dobbin ! Jip ! " Then up he sprang, and moved off, dragging the lion behind him. The beast began to roar and bellow, till all the birds of the wood flew away for fright; but the horse let him sing on, and made his way quietly over the fields to his master's house.

"Here he is, master," said he, " I have got the better of him:" nnd when the farmer saw his old servant, his heart relented, and he said " Thou shalt stay in thy stable and be well taken care of." And so the poor old horse had plenty to eat, and lived—till he died.

RUMPEL-STILTS-KIN.

In a certain kingdom once lived a poor miller who had a very beautiful daughter. She was moreover exceedingly shrewd and clever; and the miller was so vain and proud of her, that he one day told the king of the land that his daughter could spin gold out of straw. Now this king was very fond of money; and when he heard the miller's boast, his avarice was excited, and he ordered the girl to be brought before him. Then he led her to a chamber where there was a great quantity of straw, gave her a spinning-wheel, and said "All this must be spun into gold before morning, as you value your life." It was in vain that the poor maiden declared that she could do no such thing, the chamber was locked and she remained alone.

She sat down in one corner of the room and began to lament over her hard fate, when on a sudden the door opened, and a droll-looking little man hobbled in, and said "Good morrow to you, my good lass, what are you weeping for?" "Alas!" answered she, "I must spin this straw into gold, and I know not how." "What will you give me," said the little man, "to do it for you?" "My necklace," replied the maiden. He took her at her word, and sat himself down to the wheel; round about it went merrily, and presently the work was done and the gold all spun.

When the king came and saw this, he was greatly astonished and pleased; but his heart grew still more greedy of gain, and he shut up the poor miller's daughter again with a fresh task. Then she knew not what to do, and sat down once more to weep; but the little man presently opened the door, and said "What will you give me to do your task?" "The ring on my finger," replied she. So her little friend took the ring, and began to work at the wheel, till by the morning all was finished again.

The king was vastly delighted to see all this glittering treasure; but still he was not satisfied, and took the miller's daughter into a yet larger room, and said "All this must be spun to-night; and if you succeed, you shall be my queen." As soon as she was alone the dwarf came in, and said "What will you give me to spin gold for you this third time?" "I have nothing left," said she. "Then promise me," said the little man, "your first little child when you are queen." "That may never be," thought the miller's daughter: and as she knew no other way to get her task done, she promised him what he asked, and he spun once more the whole heap of gold. The king came in the morning, and finding all he wanted, married her, and so the miller's daughter really became queen.

At the birth of her first little child the queen rejoiced very much, and forgot the little man and her promise; but one day he came into her chamber and reminded her of it. Then she grieved sorely at her misfortune, and offered him all the treasures of the kingdom in exchange; but in vain, till at last her tears softened him, and he said "I will give you three days' grace, and if during that time you tell me my hame, you shall keep your child."

Now the queen lay awake all night, thinking of all the odd names that she had ever heard, and dispatched messengers all over the land to inquire after new ones. The next day the little man came, and she began with Timothy, Benjamin, Jeremiah, and all the names she could remember; but to all of them he said, "That's not my name."

The second day she began with all the comical names she could hear of, Bandy-legs, Hunch-back, Crook-shanks, and so on; but the little gentleman still said to every one of them, That's not my name."

The third day one of the messengers came back, and said "I can hear of no other names; but yesterday, as I was climbing a high hill among the trees of the forest where the fox and the hare bid each other good night, I saw a little hut, and before the hut burnt a fire, and round about the fire a funny little man danced upon one leg, and sang

> "Merrily the feast I'll make,
> To-day I'll brew, to-morrow bake;
> Merrily I'll dance and sing,
> For next day will a stranger bring:
> Little does my lady dream
> Rumpel-Stilts-kin is my name!"

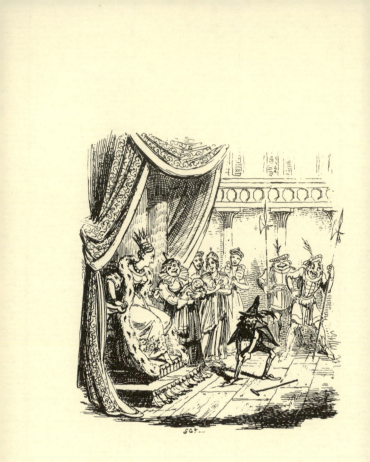

When the queen heard this, she jumped for joy, and as soon as her little visitor came, and said " Now, lady, what is my name ?" " Is it John ?" asked she. " No !" " Is it Tom ?" " No !"

" Can your name be Rumpel-stilts-kin ? "

" Some witch told you that! Some witch told you that !" cried the little man, and dashed his right foot in a rage so deep into the floor, that he was forced to lay hold of it with both hands to pull it out. Then he made the best of his way off, while every body laughed at him for having all his trouble for nothing.

L

NOTES.

Preface, p. vii.—We have another popular song to the Lady-bird under a different name,

" Bless you, bless you, Burnie-bee,
Tell me when your wedding be ;
If it be to-morrow day,
Take your wings and fly away."

Hans in Luck, p. 1.—The " Hans im Glück" of MM. Grimm ; a story of popular currency communicated by Aug. Wernicke to the *Wünschelruthe,* a periodical publication, 1818, No. 33.—A friend informs us, that this story is well known in the northern parts of England.

The Travelling Musicians, or *The Waits of Bremen,* p. 9. —The " Bremer Stadtmusikanten " of Grimm ; current in Paderborn. Rollenhagen, who in the 16th century wrote his poem called *Froschmäuseler,* (a collection of popular satirical dramatic scenes, in which animals are the acting characters,) has admirably versified the leading incidents of this story. The occupant parties who are ejected by the travellers are, with him, wild beasts, not robbers. The Germans are eminently successful in their beast stories. The origin of them it is not easy to trace : as early as the age of the Minnesingers (in the beginning of the 13th century) a collection of fables, told with great spirit and humour by Boner, was current ; but they are more Æsopian, and have not the dramatic and instructive character of the tales before us, which bear the features of the oldest Oriental fables. In later times *Reineke de Voss* seems to be the matured result of this taste, and whether originating in Germany or elsewhere, it had there its chief popularity. To that cycle belong many of the tales collected by MM. Grimm ; and accordingly the Fox is constantly present, and displays every where the same characteristics. The moral tendency of these delightful fables is almost invariably exemplary ; they always give their rewards to virtue and humanity, and afford protection to the weaker but more amiable animals, against their wily or violent aggressors. Man is sometimes introduced, but generally, as in "The Dog and the Sparrow," to his disadvantage, and for the purpose of reproof and correction.

The Golden Bird, p. 16.—" Der Goldene Vogel ;" a Hessian story ; told also with slight variations in Paderborn. The substance of this tale, in which the Golden Bird is generally called the Phœnix, is of great antiquity. Perinskiold in the catalogue to Hickes mentions the *Saga af Artus Fagra*, and describes the contents thus : " Hist. de tribus fratribus, Carolo, Vilhialmo, atque Arturo, cogn. Fagra, regis Angliæ filiis, qui ad inquirendum Phœnicem, ut eâ curaretur morbus immedicabilis patris illorum, in ultimas usque Indiæ oras missi sunt."

It appears that the same subject forms a Danish popular tale. The youngest and successful son is a character of perpetual recurrence in the German tales. He is generally despised for diminutive stature, or supposed inferiority of intellect, and passes by the contemptuous appellation of the "Dummling," of whom we shall have occasion to say more hereafter.

The Fisherman and his Wife, p. 27.—"De Fischer un siine Fru," a story in the Pomeranian Low German dialect, admirably adapted to this species of narrative, and particularly pleasing to an English ear, as bearing a remarkable affinity to his own language, or rather that of the Lowland Scotch. Take the second sentence as a specimen: "Daar satt he eens an de see, bi de angel, un sach in dat blanke water, un he sach immer (ever) na de angel," &c. During the fervour of popular feeling on the downfall of the power of the late Emperor of France, this tale became a great favourite. In the original the last object of the wife's desires is to be as "de lewe Gott" (der liebe Gott, le bon Dieu). We have softened the boldness of the lady's ambition.

The Tomtit and the Bear, p. 38 —"Der Zaunkönig und der Bär;" from Zwehrn. We have Reynard here in his proper character, and the smaller animals triumphing by superior wit over the larger, in the same manner as in many of the Northern traditions the dwarfs obtain a constant superiority over their opponents the giants. In *Tuhti Nameh's* eighth fable [Calcutta and London, 1801], an elephant is punished for an attack upon the sparrow's nest, by an alliance which she forms with another bird, a frog, and a bee.

The Twelve Dancing Princesses, p. 43.—" Die zer-
tanzten Schuhe;" a Munster tale; known also with variations in other parts, and even in Poland, according
to the report made by Dobrowsky to MM. Grimm.
The story is throughout of a very Oriental cast, except
that the soldier has the benefit of the truly Northern
Nebel, or Tarn-kappe, which makes the wearer invisible. It should be observed, however, that in the Calmuck *Relations of Ssidi Kur* we have the cap, the
wearer of which is " seen neither by the gods nor men,
nor Tchadkurrs," and also the swiftly moving boots or
shoes.

Rose-Bud, p 51.—" Dornröschen ;" a Hessian story.
We have perhaps in our alteration of the heroine's name
lost one of the links of connexion, which M. Grimm
observe between this fable and that of the ancient tradition of the restoration of Brynhilda, by Sigurd, as
narrated in the *Edda* of Sæmund, in *Volsunga Saga*.
Sigurd pierces the enchanted fortifications, and rouses
the heroine. "Who is it," said she, " of might sufficient
to rend my armour and to break my sleep ? " She afterwards tells the cause of her trance: " Two kings con-
tended ; one hight Hialmgunnar, and he was old but of
mickle might, and Odin had promised him the victory.
I felled him in fight; but Odin struck my head with the
sleepy-thorn, [the Thorn-rose or Dog-rose, see *Alt-
deutsche Walder*, I. 135.] and said I should never be
again victorious, and should be hereafter wedded." Herbert's *Miscell. Poetry*, vol. ii. p. 23. Though the allusion to the sleep-rose is preserved in our heroine's
name, she suffers from the wound of a spindle, as in the
Pentamerone of G. B. Basile, V. 5. The further pro-

gress of Sigurd's, or Siegfried's, adventures will be seen in " The King of the Golden Mountain."

Tom Thumb, p. 57.—The " Daumesdick " of Grimm, from Mühlheim, on the Rhine. In this tale the hero appears in his humblest domestic capacity ; but there are others in which he plays a most important and heroic character, as the outwitter and vanquisher of giants and other powerful enemies, the favourite of fortune, and the winner of the hands of kings' daughters. We should have been glad, if it had been consistent with the immediate design of this publication, to have given two or three other stories from different parts of Germany, illustrative of the worth and ancient descent of the personage who appears with the same general characteristics, under the various names in England of Tom Thumb, Tom-a-lyn, Tamlane, Tommel-finger, &c. ; in Germany of Daumesdick, Däumling, Daumerling and Dummling (for though the latter word bears a different and independent meaning, we incline to think it originally the same); in Austria of Daumenlang; in Denmark of Svend Tomling, or Swain Tomling; and further north, as the Thaumlin, or dwarfish hero of Scandinavia.

We must refer to the *Quarterly Review*, No. xli., for a speculation as to the connexion of Tom's adventures, particularly that with the cow, with some of the mysteries of Indian mythology. It must suffice here briefly to notice the affinities which some of the present stories bear to the earliest Northern traditions, leaving the reader to determine whether, as Hearne concludes, our hero was King Edgar's page, or, as tradition says, ended his course and found his last home at Lincoln.

In one of the German stories, "Des Schneiders Daumerling Wanderschaft," (the Travels of the Tailor's
Thumbling,) his first wandering is through the re-
cesses of a glove, to escape his mother's anger. So
Thor, in the 23rd fable of the *Edda*, reposes in the
giant's glove. In another story, " Der junge Riese"
(The young Giant), the hero is in his youth a thumb
long ; but, being nurtured by a giant, acquires wonderful power, and passes through a variety of adventures,
resembling at various times those of Siegfried, or Sigurd,
(the doughty champion, who according to the Heldenbuch " caught the lions in the woods and hung them
over the walls by their tails"), of Thor, and of Grettir (the
hero who kept geese on the common), and correspond-
ing with the achievements ascribed in England to his
namesake, to Jack the Giant-killer, and Tom Hycophric
(whose sphere of action Hearne would limit to the
contracted boundaries of Tylney in Norfolk), and in the
Servian tale, quoted by MM. Grimm from Schottky,
given to " the son of the bear," Medvedovitsh.

He serves the smith, whose history as the Velint (or
Weyland) of Northern fable is well known ; outwits,
like Eulen-spiegel (Owl-glass), those who are by nature his betters ; wields a weapon as powerful as
Thor's hammer ; and, like his companion, is somewhat
impregnable to tolerably rude attacks. He is equally
voracious, too, with Loke, whose " art consisted in eating more than any other man in the world," and with
the son of Odin, when " busk'd as a bride so fair," in
the *Song of Thrym*,

> " Betimes at evening he approached,
>   And the mantling ale the giants broached ;

> The spouse of Sifia ate alone
> Eight salmons and an ox full grown,
> And all the cates on which women feed,
> And drank three firkins of sparkling mead."
>
> HERBERT's *Icelandic Poetry*, i. p. 6.

In one of the tales before us, a mill-stone is treacherously thrown upon him while employed in digging at the bottom of a well. " Drive away the hens," said he ; " they scratch the sand about till it flies into my eyes." So in the *Edda*, the Giant Skrymmer only notices the dreadful blows of Thor's hammer as the falling of a leaf, or some other trifling matter. In the English story of *Jack the Giant-killer*, Jack under similar circumstances says, that a rat had given him three or four slaps with his tail.

In the story of "The King of the Golden Mountain," it will be seen how the giants are outwitted and deprived of the great Northern treasures, the tarn-kap, the shoes, and the sword, which are equally renowned in the records of the *Niebelungen-lied* and *Niflunga Saga*, and in our own *Jack the Giant-killer*. The other Thumb tales are full of such adventures. They are all exceedingly curious, and deserve to be brought together in one view as forming a singular group. At present we can only refer to the pages of MM. Grimm, and particularly to the observations in their notes.

The Grateful Beasts, p. 68.—" Die treuen Thiere ;" from the Schwalmgegend, in Hesse. It is singular that nearly the same story is to be found in the *Relations of Ssidi Kur,* a collection of tales current among the Calmuck Tartars. A benevolent Bramin

L 5

there receives the grateful assistance of a mouse, a bear, and a monkey, whom he has severally rescued from the hands of their tormentors ; *Quarterly Review*, No. xli. p. 99. There is a very similar story, " Lo Scarafone, lo Sorece, e lo Grillo," in the *Pentamerone*, iii. 5. Another in the same work, iv. 1, " La Preta de lo Gallo," embraces the incidents of the latter part of our tale. The *Gesta Romanorum* also contains a fable somewhat similar in plot, though widely different in details. The cunning device of the mouse reminds MM. Grimm of Loke, in the form of a fly, stinging the sleeping Freya till she throws off her necklace.

Jorinda and Jorindel, p 75.—" Jorinde und Joringel." This is taken from *Heinrich Stillings Leben*, i. 104—108 ; but a story of precisely the same nature is popular in the Schwalmgegend.

The Waggish Musician, p. 81.—" Der Wunderliche Spielmann," from Lorsch, by Worms. The story seems imperfect, as no reason appears for the spite of the musician towards the animals who follow his Orphean strains.

The Queen Bee, p. 86.—" Die Bienen-königin;" from Hesse ; where another story of similar plot is current. The resemblance to that of " The Grateful Beasts," will of course be obvious. We have here the favourite incident of the despised and neglected member of the family, who bears the name of "Dummling," setting out on his adventures, and overcoming all disadvantages by talent and virtue. (See note on " The Golden Goose," in which story we have left the hero his name, as perhaps we ought to have done here.) MM. Grimm mention a Jewish tale of Rabbi Chanina who befriends a raven, a hound, and a fish, and receives similar tokens of gratitude. In the Hungarian stories, collected from popular narration by Georg von Gaal, (Vienna, 1822,) there is one (No. 8.) to the same effect. The incident of picking up the pearls will remind the reader of the task of Psyche, in *Apuleius*, lib. vi., in which she is assisted by the ants.

The Dog and the Sparrow, p. 90.—" Der Hund und der Sperling ;" told with variations in Zwehrn, Hesse, and Göttingen.

Frederick and Catherine, p. 96.—" Der Frieder und das Catherlieschen;" from Zwehrn and Hesse. Some of the incidents in this story are to be found in that of Bardiello, in the *Pentamerone*, i. 4. We have frequently heard it told in our younger days as a popular story in England.

The Three Children of Fortune, p. 106.—" Die drei Glückskinder;" from Paderborn. It is not necessary to point out the coincidence of one of the adventures of this story with that of Whittington, once Lord Mayor of London. But it is not merely in Germany that the same tale is traced. " We learn from Mr. Morier's entertaining narrative that Whittington's cat realized its price in India." In Italy, the merry priest Arlotto told the story in his *Facezie*, before the Lord Mayor was born or thought of ; he describes the adventure as happening to a Geneway merchant, and adds that another upon hearing of the profitable adventure made a voyage to Rat Island with a precious cargo, for which the king repaid him with one of the cats.—*Quarterly Review*, XLI. p. 100.

King Grisly-beard, p. 111.—" König Drosselbart;" from Hesse, the Main and Paderborn. The story of " La Soperbia castecata," *Pentamerone*, iv. 10, has a similar turn. There are of course many other tales in different countries, having for their burthen " The Taming of the Shrew." It hardly need be observed that our title is not meant as a *translation* of the German name.

Chanticleer and Partlet, p. 118. — This comprizes three stories, " Das Lumpengesindel," " Herr Korbes," and " Von dem Tod des Hühnchens," from Paderborn, the Main and Hesse, placed together as naturally forming one continuous piece of biography. We shall perhaps be told that the whole is tolerably childish; but we wished to give a specimen of each variety of these tales, and at the same time an instance of the mode in which inanimate objects are pressed into the service. The death of Hühnchen forms a balladized story published in *Wunderhorn*, vol. iii., among the Kinderlieder. Who " Herr Korbes" is, or what his name imports, we know not; and we should therefore observe that we have of our own authority alone turned him into an enemy, and named him " the fox," in order to give some sort of reason for the outrage committed on his hospitality by uninvited guests.

Snow-drop, p. 128.—" Sneewitchen;" told with several minor variations in Hesse ; also at Vienna with more important alterations. In one version, Spiegel (the glass) is the name of a dog, who performs the part of the queen's monitor. The wish of the queen which opens this story has been illustrated in the *Alt-deutsche Walder,* vol. i. p. 1, in a dissertation on a curious passage in Wolfram von Eschenbach's romance of *Parcifal,* where the hero bursts forth into a pathetic allusion to his lady's charms on seeing drops of blood fallen on snow,

> " Trois gotes de fres sanc
> Qui enluminoient le blanc,"

as Chretien de Troyes expresses it in the French romance on the same subject ;

> " —— panse tant, qu'il s'oblie ;
> Ausins estoit en son avis
> Li vermauz sor le blanc asis,
> Come les gotes de sanc furent,
> Qui desor le blanc aparurent;
> Au l'esgarder, que il faisoit,
> Li est avis, tant li pleisoit,
> Qu'il veist la color novelle
> De la face s'amie belle."

Several parallel wishes are selected from the ancient traditionary stories of different countries, from the Irish legend of Deirda and Navis, the son of Visneach, in Keating's *History of Ireland,* to the Neapolitan stories in *Pentamerone,* iv. 9. & v. 8.

" O cielo! " says the hero in the latter, " e non porria havere un mogliere acossi janco, e rossa, comme e chella preta, e che havesse li capello e le ciglia acossi negro, comme fo le penne di chisto cuervo," &c. The unfading corpse placed in the glass coffin is to be found also in the *Pentamerone*, ii. 8. (la Schiavottella): and in *Haralds Saga*, Snäfridr his beauteous wife dies, but her countenance changes not, its bloom continuing ; and the king sits by the body watching it three years.

The dwarfs who appear in this story are of genuine Northern descent. They are Metallarii, live in mountains, and are of the benevolent class ; for it must be particularly observed that this, and the mischievous race, are clearly distinguishable. The *Heldenbuch* says, " God produced the dwarfs because the mountains lay waste and useless, and valuable stores of silver and gold with gems and pearls were concealed in them. Therefore he made them right wise, and crafty, that they could distinguish good and bad, and to what use all things should be applied. They knew the use of gems ; that some of them gave strength to the wearer, others made him invisible, which were called fog-caps ; therefore God gave art and wisdom to them, that they built them hollow hills," &c. (*Illustrations of Northern Antiquities*, p. 41.) The most beautiful example of the ancient Teutonic romance is that which contains the adventures, and the description of the abode in the mountains, of Laurin the King of the Dwarfs. Those who wish to obtain full and accurate information on the various species, habits and manners of these sons of the mountains, may consult Olaus Magnus, or, at far greater length, the *Anthropodemus Plutonicus* of Prætorius.

We ought to observe that this story has been somewhat shortened by us, the style of telling it in the original being rather diffuse ; and we have not entered into the particulars of the queen's death, which in the German is occasioned by the truly Northern punishment of being obliged to dance in red-hot slippers or shoes.

The Elves and the Shoemaker, p. 140.—" Die Wichtelmanner—von einem Schuster dem sie die Arbeit gemacht," a Hessian tale. We have no nomenclature sufficiently accurate for the classification of the goblin tribes of the North. The personages now before us are of the benevolent and working class ; they partake of the general character given of such personages by Olaus Magnus, and of the particular qualities of the Housemen (Hausmänner), for whose history we must refer to *Prætorius,* cap. viii. These sprites were of a very domestic turn, attaching themselves to particular households, very pleasant inmates when favourably disposed, very troublesome when of a mischievous temperament, and generally expecting some share of the good things of the family as a reward for services which they were not accustomed to give gratuitously. " The drudging goblin" works, but does so

> " To earn his cream-bowl duly set,
> When in one night, e'er glimpse of morn,
> His shadowy flail had thresh'd the corn,
> That ten day labourers could not end."
> Milton, *L'Allegro.*

The Turnip, p. 143.—" Die Rübe." The first part of this story is well known. The latter part is the subject of an old Latin poem of the 14th century, entitled " Raparius" (who was probably the versifier), existing

in MS. at Strasburg, and also at Vienna.   MM.
Grimm think they see, through the comic dress of
this story, various allusions to ancient Northern traditions, and they particularly refer to the wise man
(*Runa capituli*), who imbibes knowledge in his airy sus-
pension.

> Veit ek, at ek hiek vindga meidi a
> Nätur allar niu.
> Tha nam ek frevaz ok frodr vera.

" I know that I hung on the wind-agitated tree nine
full nights ; there began I to become—wise."

Old Sultan, p. 149.—" Der alte Sultan;" from Hesse
and Paderborn ; in four versions, each varying in some
slight particulars.

The Lady and the Lion, p. 153.—" Das singende,
springende Löweneckerchen ;" from Hesse. Another
version with variations comes from the Schwalmgegend,
and from this latter we have taken the opening incident of the summer and winter garden, in preference to
the parallel adventure in the story which MM. Grimm
have adopted in their text. We have made two or three
other alterations in the way of curtailment of portions of
the story. The common tale of " Beauty and the Beast "
has always some affinity to the legend of Cupid and
Psyche. In the present version of the same fable the
resemblance is striking throughout. The poor heroine pays the price of her imprudence in being compelled to wander over the world in search of her husband ; she goes to heavenly powers for assistance in
her misfortunes, and at last, when within reach of the

object of her hopes, is near being defeated by the al-
lurements of pleasure. Mrs. Tighe's beautiful poem
would seem purposely to describe some of the immediate incidents of our tale, particularly that of the
dove.

The incidents in which the misfortune originates are
to be found in *Pentamerone* ii. 9 (Lo Catenaccio), and
still further in v. 4 (Lo Turzo d'Oro). The scene in the
bridegroom's chamber is in *Pentam.* v. 3 (Pintosmauto).
Prætorius, ii. p. 266, gives a Beauty and the Beast story
from Sweden.

The Jew in the Bush, p. 163.—" Der Jude im Dorn."
The dance-inspiring instrument will be recognised, in
its most romantic and dignified form, as Oberon's Horn
in *Huon de Bordeaux.* The dance in the bush forms
the subject of two old German dramatic pieces of the
16th century. A disorderly monk occupies the place
of the Jew; the waggish musician is called Dulla,
whom MM. Grimm connect with Tyll or Dill Eulen-
spiegel (Owl-glass), and the Swedish and Scandinavian word, Thulr, (facetus, nugator,) the clown and
minstrel of the populace. In *Herrauds ok Bosa Saga,*
the table, chairs, &c. join the dance. Merlin in the
old romance is entrapped into a bush, by a charm given
him by his mistress Viviane.

In England we have *A mery Geste of the Frere and
the Boye,* first " emprynted at London in Flete-streete,
at the sygne of the Sonne, by Wynkyn de Worde,"
and edited by Ritson in his *Pieces of ancient popular
Poetry.* The boy receives

————" a bowe
Byrdes for to shete,"

and a pipe of marvellous power :

> "All that may the pype here
>   Shall not themselfe stere,
>   But laugh and lepe aboute."

The third gift is a most special one for the annoyance of his stepdame. The dancing trick is first played on a "Frere," who loses

> " His cope and his scapelary
>   And all his other wede."

And the urchin's ultimate triumph is over the "offy-cyall" before whom he is brought.

The King of the Golden Mountain, p. 169. —"Der König vom Goldenen Berg ;" from Zwehrn and other quarters. There are many remarkable features in this story, more especially its striking resemblance to the story of Sigurd or Siegfried, as it is to be collected from the *Edda,* the *Volsunga Saga, Wilkina Saga,* the *Niebelungen Lied,* and the popular tale of *The Horny Siegfried.* It is neatly abridged in Herbert's *Misc. Poetry,* vol. ii. part ii. p. 14. The placing upon the waters ; the arrival at the castle of the dragon or snake ; the treasures there ; the disenchantment of Brynhilda (see our tale of Rose-Bud) ; the wishing ring ; the gift of the ring or girdle ; the separation from which jealousy and mischief are to flow ; the disguise of the old cloak, which we can easily believe to have been a genuine tarn-cap ; the encountering of the discordant guardians of the treasures, as in the *Niebelungen Lied*; the wonderful sword Balmung or Mimung ;

> " (Thro' hauberk as thro' harpelon
>   The smith's son swerd shall hew ; *)"

---

* " Ettin Langshanks," translated from the *Kümpe Visir* in the *Illustrations of Northern Antiquities.*

the boots " once worn by Loke when he escaped from
Valhalla;" and the ultimate revenge; are all points
more or less coincident with adventures well known to
those who have made the old fables of the North the
objects of their researches. It should be recollected,
however, that both the cap of invisibility and the boots
of swiftness are to be found in the *Relations of Ssidi
Kur*. The Hungarian tales published by Georg von Gaal,
Vienna, 1822, contain one very similar to this in many
particulars. Three dwarfs are there the inheritors of
the wonderful treasures, which consist of a cloak, mile-
shoes, and a purse which is always full.

The Golden Goose, p. 178.—" Die Goldene Gans ;"
from Hesse and Paderborn. " The manner in which
Loke, in the *Edda*, hangs to the eagle is," MM. Grimm
observe, " better understood after a perusal of the
story of the Golden Goose, to which the lads and lasses
who touch it adhere."—*Quart. Rev.* XLI. They add that
the Golden Goose, buried at the root of an oak, and
fated to be the reward of virtue, and to bring blessing
on its owner, seems only one of the various types by
which, in these tales, happiness, wealth and power, are
conferred on the favourites of fortune. The prize is
here poetically described as so attractive, that whatever
approaches clings to it as to a magnet.

The Dummling is drawn with his usual characteristics ; he is sometimes inferior in stature, sometimes in
intellect, and at other times in both ; his resemblance
to the Däumling or Thumbling is obvious; and though
his name has now an independent meaning, perhaps
we should suspect it to have been originally the same ;
unless the appearance of the character in the *Penta-*

merone iii. 8, by the unambiguous name of " Lo Gno-
rante," be against our theory. We leave this singular
personage in the hands of MM. Grimm, referring also
to the *Altdeutsche Walder*, where our hero is pointed
out as appearing under the appellation of " Dumme-
klare" in the romance of *Parcifal*.

Mrs. Fox, p. 184.—"Von der Frau Füchsin." A popular fable in several places, clearly belonging to the
class of which Reynard the Fox is the chief.

Hansel and Grettel, p. 188.—The first part of " Brü-
derchen und Schwesterchen;" the remainder we omitted
as branching into a new series of distinct adventures.
The story is very common in Germany, and is also known
in Sweden. Prætorius, vol. ii., p. 255, will give the
curious the whole art, mystery and history, of trans-
formation of men into animals. This story is one of a
most numerous class, in which a stepmother unsuccess-
fully exerts a malicious influence over her charge.

The Giant with the three Golden Hairs, p. 195.—" Der
Teufel mit den drei Goldnen Haaren;" from Zwehrn,
the Main and Hesse. We have taken the appellation
"Giant" to avoid offence, and felt less reluctance in
the alteration when we found that some other versions
of the same story (as the Popanz in *Büsching's Volks-
sagen)* omit the diabolic agency. For similar reasons
we have not called the cave by its proper name of
" Hölle," the Scandinavian Hell. The old lady called
in the German the " Eller-mutter," we suspect has
some connexion with the Scandinavian deity " Hela,"
or " Hella," whom Odin, (when he " saddled straight

his coal-black steed,") Hermod Huat, and Brynhilda, after crossing the water as here, severally found in the same position, at the entrance of the infernal regions.

The child is described in our translation as owing its reputation to being born under a lucky star. In the original it is born with a Glückshaut (caul). The tradition in Iceland is that a good genius dwells in this envelope, who accompanies and blesses the child through life. The giant's powers of scent will of course remind the curious reader of the

> " Snouk but, Snouk ben,
> I find the smell of earthly men,"

in *Jack and the Bean-stalk.*

So in Mad Tom's ballad in Shakespeare,

> " Child Rowland to the dark tower came—
> His word was still—Fie, Foh, Fum,
> I smell the blood of a British man," &c.

Is Child Rowland the " liebste Roland " of the German popular story, No. 56 of MM. Grimm's collection ? The similarity of the "Child's" adventures with those of Danish ballads in the *Kämpe Viser* has been pointed out by Jamieson in his *Popular Ballads,* and in the *Illustrations of Northern Antiquities,* p. 397.

The Frog-prince, p. 205.—" Der Froschkönig, oder der Eiserne Heinrich." This story is from Hesse, but is also told in other parts with variations. It is one of the oldest German tales, as well as of extensive currency elsewhere. Dr. Leyden gives a story of the " Frog-lover " as popular in Scotland. A lady is sent

by her step-mother to draw water from the Well of the
World's End.   She arrives at the well after encountering many dangers, but soon perceives that her adventures have not reached a conclusion; a frog emerges
from the well, and before it suffers her to draw water
obliges her to betroth herself to him under penalty of
being torn to pieces. The lady returns safe; but at midnight the frog-lover appears at the door and demands
entrance, according to promise, to the great consterna-
tion of the lady and her nurse.

> " Open the door, my hinny, my heart,
>   Open the door, mine ain wee thing;
>   And mind the words that you and I spak
>   Down in the meadow by the well-spring."

The frog is admitted, and addresses her,

> " Take me upon your knee, my dearie,
>   Take me upon your knee, my dearie,
>   And mind the words that you and I spak
>   At the cauld well sae weary."

The frog is finally disenchanted, and appears as a
prince, in his original form. (See *Complaint of Scotland*,
Edin. 1801.) " These enchanted frogs," says the Quarterly Reviewer, " have migrated from afar, and we suspect that they were originally crocodiles : we trace
them in *The Relations of Ssidi Kur*." The name
" Iron Henry" in the German title alludes to an incident which we have omitted, though it is one of considerable antiquity.   The story proceeds to tell how
Henry, from grief at his master's misfortune, had bound
his heart with iron bands to prevent its bursting; and a
doggrel is added, in which the prince on his journey,

hearing the cracking of the bands which his servant is now rending asunder as useless, inquires if the carriage is breaking, and receives an explanation of the cause of the disturbance.

> " Heinrich, der Wagen bricht ! "
> " Nein, Herr, der Wagen nicht :
> Es ist ein Band von meinem Herzen,
> Das da lag in grossen Schmerzen,
> Als ihr in dem Brunnen sast
> Als ihr eine Fretsche (Frosch) wast.

In several of the poets of the age of the Minnesingers the suffering heart is described as confined in bands ; " stahelhart," according to Heinrich von Sax.

The Fox and Horse, p. 210.—" Der Fuchs und das Pferd ;" from Munster. See the story of " Old Sultan."

Rumpel-stilts-kin, p 217.—" Rumpelstilzchen." A story of considerable currency, told with several variations. We remember to have heard a similar story from Ireland in which the song ran,

> " Little does my Lady wot
> That my name is Trit-a-Trot."

In the " Tour tenebreuse et les jours lumineux, Contes Anglois tirez d'une ancienne chronique composée par Richard surnommé Cœur de Lion, Roy d'Angleterre, Amst. 1708," the story of " Ricdin-Ricdon" contains the same incident. The song of the dwarf is as follows :

" Si jeune et tendre femelle
    N'aimant qu'enfantins ebats,
    Avoit mis dans sa cervelle
    Que Ricdin-Ricdon, je m'appelle,
    Point ne viendroit dans mes laqs :
    Mais sera pour moi la belle
    Car un tel nom ne sçait pas."

There is a good deal of learned and mythologic speculation in MM. Grimm, as to the spinning of gold, for
which we must refer the reader to their work. The
dwarf has here, as usual, his abode in the almost inac-
cessible part of the mountains. In the original he rends
himself asunder in his efforts to extricate the foot
which in his rage he had struck into the ground.

THE END.